MW00896075

THE
GENERAL'S
BRIDE

For you dear Valerie
with my affection

Ilona
Jan 2018

THE
GENERAL'S
BRIDE

ILONA COLE

Library of Congress Control Number:		2017918375
ISBN:	Hardcover	978-1-5434-6973-8
	Softcover	978-1-5434-6972-1
	eBook	978-1-5434-6971-4

This is a work of fiction based on a true story.

Print information available on the last page.

Rev. date: 12/07/2017

To order additional copies of this book, contact:
Xlibris
1-888-795-4274
www.Xlibris.com
Orders@Xlibris.com
769676

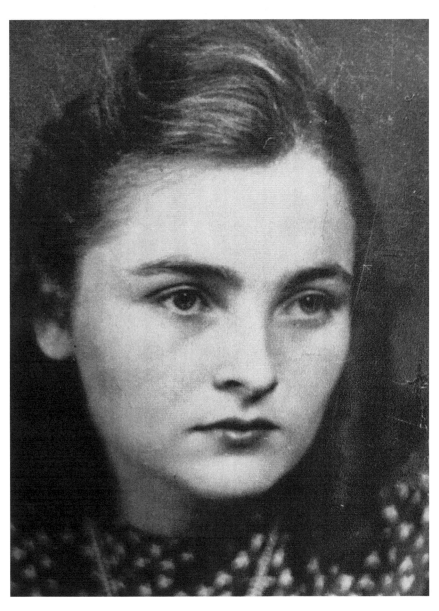

The General's Bride, Elisabetha "Lizzi" age 21

In memory of my beloved husband, Halvor LeGrand Cole, who wanted me to write this story many years ago. With my everlasting love for him, I present

THE GENERAL'S BRIDE

ACKNOWLEDGEMENTS

With my profound appreciation and thanks to Marcie Sims for her support and everlasting help to me to complete *The General's Bride.*

My thanks and appreciation to Traci Cole for the beautiful sketches of the Trakehner, "Maxi," and the twelve metre sloop, "ANMUT."

My thanks to Beverly Florence for her support throughout the production process.

A profound thanks to Xlibris and their support teams;

Toni Sales

Emman Villaran and

Harriet Jimenez who was a great help and support throughout the final progress of the book.

The design team who worked hard to make this beautiful cover.

My sincere thanks.

The First World War has come to an end for the beautiful Elisabetha (her father called her his Lizzi when he was tender with her). Her married life had started in 1920. She was sitting on her favorite bench by the rose garden, very happy, and wondering if she were dreaming that all this which is surrounding her could actually be true: this grand and so beautiful house with an enormous manicured rose garden and the kind and handsome husband—no, she never wanted to wake up. In this rose garden on a sunny afternoon, she spent her time sitting on a bench by the fountain, breathing in the heavenly fragrance of white and red roses while daydreaming.

In thought, Lizzi went back to her home, her childhood, and her young adulthood, when her older sister Frieda and she would be ever so excited when an invitation from the grand duke and duchess for a formal ball would arrive. They, Lizzi and her two sisters, dreamed of getting all dressed up.

Their gowns were custom-made for each sister individually, but each one was different. For the Christmas ball, Frieda's gown of burgundy velvet, befitting her auburn hair, was long and graceful, hugging her slender shape. The sleeves were long, the back was low-cut, and she wore a beautiful necklace of rubies, having it fall down her low-cut back.

Lizzi's gown fitted also of a beautiful coffee-brown silk crepe, a warm and wonderful combination to her auburn hair. The skirt of the dress was full and long, looking great on the dance floor. The bodice of the dress was fitted and embroidered with gold metal thread in an arabesque design, with square neckline and slender long sleeves to minimize the fullness of the skirt. She wore no jewelry, due to the beautiful embroidery, but on each ear, she wore a gorgeous diamond stud.

Their youngest sister, Katja, entered the ball in a lovely gown of dark emerald-green taffeta with a long, full skirt and tight bodice with rounded décolleté. As a little soft touch, she wore a dark emerald-green velvet ribbon around her neck with a beautiful cameo decorating her décolleté. The warm dark green color of her dress suited her curly red hair.

The three sisters, in stunning gowns, entered the grand ballroom together. Other debutants—also in a variety of beautiful gowns in white, many in red, and a few very striking in black—all entered the ballroom, and the handsome young officers greeted them and asked for this dance. Lizzi's heart was beating faster when she again envisioned herself falling in love with this handsome cavalry officer, August, who just returned from a British prisoner-of-war camp in what was then called Ceylon by India. Now it is Sri Lanka. August was very handsome, with black hair and blue eyes, and he was tall. Clearly, she saw herself as a bride and happily envisioned her beautiful wedding in this stately home and this very endearing rose garden.

Lizzi also remembers clearly that special ball—the arrival of some special guests announced by the grand duke and duchess, when she saw and danced for the first time with that handsome August. How well he danced and how he looked at her. She wondered that evening how a kiss would feel should he want to kiss her. That evening, Lizzi did not find out, but she must have made an impression on this handsome one. When the next ball was announced, Lizzi was all excited and nervous, wondering if August would be there again and if he would remember her. She wore a striking emerald-green silk ball gown, tight fitted to show off her small waist, straight-cut in the front, and gathered on a bias in the back from the waist down. She was very stunning with her auburn hair pulled back into a chignon, held by a comb adorned with five emeralds. No other jewelry was needed. She looked beautiful standing by the entryway with Frieda and Katja looking around the ballroom.

She spotted August, his eyes searching the dance floor. Not seeing what he was looking for, he started to walk away. As he did, he noticed the three sisters by the entry and approached them with a smile on his face. He bowed and kissed Lizzi's hand. His beautiful blue eyes looked up at her with an admiring glance. He smiled at her and took her hand to guide her to the dance floor. They danced again all evening, though several times they took time out to go outside to the terrace to talk. That evening, not only was August telling Lizzi about himself, how he came to be living in Darmstadt, and about his father, but also Lizzi, the inquisitive one, found out what feeling she would have when he kissed her. She was on a cloud that evening and was still on that cloud when the three sisters were picked up to come home.

Lizzi was a beautiful and lovely bride, her gown of white Chantilly lace and veil with a precious, old cameo, set in gold filigree, adorning her throat. August, walking beside her, was a tall and handsome former cavalry officer, dressed in formal attire. Under his classic well-fitting tuxedo, he wore a white silk shirt with fine pleats down the button front and around his neck a beautiful black-and-white silk ribbon that held his grand Pour le Mérite, not only the highest medal given to officers in World War I but also the most sought-after and beautiful medal ever given for valor and heroism in World War I: the medal's design was a cross in brilliant blue porcelain, framed in twenty-four-karat gold, with gold filigree behind the cross.

August, The General

They were a beautiful and elegant couple walking up the stairs, past the guests, and across a threshold covered with rose petals into his house.

Coming through a large and beautiful iron gate, a walkway with wide stairs flanked by tall Asian pots filled with flowers led to the front of a stately grand white stucco home. A heavy double door led into an elegant two-story-high foyer. Coming down from the center high above was a most beautiful chandelier. In the far corner, partially under the wide curved stairway, was a grand piano. In the center of the foyer was a big round marble-topped table that held a Lalique vessel with the last gorgeous white roses. Double doors of exquisitely carved wood led to all the rooms around the foyer. Toward the back corner was the entry to the kitchen, large and well-appointed, Lizzi's favorite room. Crossing the foyer were three double doors that led to the dining room, the living room, and August's library. There were high ceilings in all rooms and high French windows. All floors had inlaid solid wood in high-gloss finish laid in a star pattern in the center. Some rooms had precious oriental carpets, and some, like the dining room, showed the beautiful design on the floor. A nice French window above the entry with a little balcony outside gave light to the upstairs landing, winding all around the second floor, with carved double doors leading to all the bedrooms and bath. By the side of the manicured property, through an ornate iron gate, wide stairs would lead to the house.

In the summer, the trellis, full of fragrant roses covering the wide stairs, made a tunnel. The back of this stately home covered in ivy had, on the first floor, a sandstone-covered terrace, and each room facing had large French windows overlooking this terrace. On the second floor was a balcony with an ornate iron railing across all windows. If Lizzi thought this to be a wonderful garden, she was amazed more so by the inside of this elegant home, built in 1889 when August's father came from Potsdam, Prussia, to Darmstadt, at the request of the grand duke in Darmstadt. It was also the year August and his twin brother, Arthur, were born.

Still daydreaming, Lizzi was thinking of the times in the beginning when she and Frieda would eagerly await the next invitation for a formal dance at the castle and anticipate if he, the handsome one, would be there again. Would he dance with her again? How heartbroken would she be if he were not there or if he was dancing the evening away with another? Frieda had not yet found her heartthrob; no one yet gave her that extra heartbeat.

Lizzi dreamed of the green meadows with colorful wildflowers surrounding a charming village. Black iron gas lanterns line both sides of the main street leading to a plaza with a large fountain in the center. This was the starting point of five streets with restaurants, outdoor dining, and beautiful shops leading away from the fountain. On a summer's evening, a romantic spot was around the fountain for the young, whereas the benches around the plaza were the meeting and resting place for the old.

Lizzi again saw herself and her two sisters—Frieda, the eldest, and the red-headed Katrina (called Katja), the youngest—by the fountain, each tossing a coin into the water and making a wish. Now Lizzi knows that her wish has come true. She had a beautiful smile on her face but did not wake up. The first thing to think about though was their education: finishing school in Switzerland and then a culinary academy in France to complete their education so they could be prepared to become the perfect wife and hostess someday. Had the coins brought love and happiness only to Lizzi and not to Frieda or Katja? While at the ball, the three sisters, beautiful and poised, had many dance partners, but no one stood out for Frieda whom she might have that extra heartbeat for.

But everything changed one Saturday night during Christmas season. The grand duke and duchess hosted a special ball. The grand duke had a guest he introduced as they entered the ballroom: "Freiherr von Walde." He was a very handsome and elegant gentleman, a count, not in uniform, but in civilian clothing. Frieda, standing next to Lizzi, whispered his name a few times as she admired this guest, and Lizzi knew at that moment that Frieda felt that extra heartbeat for him. Later, Frieda blushed when Christopher von Walde walked toward their table to ask her for that dance. The entire evening, Frieda was his dance partner. The gentleman von Walde was a breeder of a distinct breed of horses, and he came from Calau to deliver horses to the grand duke for his private cavalry regiment.

Christopher and Frieda's courtship began, but he lived quite a distance from Frieda. After some time, Christopher invited Frieda, accompanied by a chaperone, to come and stay at his grand estate not far from Berlin—in Calau, where he had his breeding farm. After some time, they fell in love; and after a beautiful wedding, Frieda moved to Calau. Lizzi realized then that Frieda's wish by the fountain had also come true. Katja no longer attended the ball at the castle by herself. She was quite a bit younger than her sisters, and she was shy.

Christopher and Frieda's wedding was a spectacular one orchestrated right in Frieda's parents' home out on the meadow under flowering peach trees. Tables and chairs were set up for the guests, who enjoyed champagne, little sandwiches, and later, the most beautiful wedding cake. Christopher was dressed in his stunning white dress uniform, a beautiful dress sword down his side. Frieda's gown was made out of yards and yards of white silk combined with lace and a long train. She looked so beautiful. It was breathtaking. They were a regal couple.

*   *   *   *

Frieda, Lizzi, and Katja's father, a well-known landowner, had dealings with many young men in the same business, and one of these young men, Philip, who took over his father's business, needed their father's advice. Many meetings were planned to complete Philip's knowledge in order to step into his father's footsteps, but Philip kept coming with the pretense of having more questions. Katja's father realized that Philip did not need his advice any longer, but he came to see his lovely daughter Katja. Her father then invited Philip to dinner, and Katja's mother continued this custom.

The two started a courtship that lasted two years and ended with a beautiful outdoor wedding in July. It was a romantic setting under the peach trees, with tables and chairs in a white tent and live music for dancing. Lizzi believed Katja's coin also brought her love and happiness. Katja's gown was made from white taffeta. It was slender and tight fitting on her petite body with a wide matching taffeta wrap draped around her shoulders. The sleeves were puffed by the shoulders and came down her arms slender and tied, buttoned with pearl buttons. Pearl buttons also adorned the dress down the back. She looked absolutely lovely. Philip, a tall and very slender man, was dressed in a tuxedo with tails. He looked very handsome. They were a beautiful and happy couple coming from the house along a path to the beautiful meadows sprinkled with wildflowers.

Lizzi's own wedding comes to her now in her dreams, and she remembers the beautiful and special gift her father gave to her and August—a once-in-a-lifetime trip not many couples were fortunate enough to make. It was a trip on the Orient Express 1883–1914, from Paris to Istanbul and back. From the 1920s to the 1930s, the carriages of the Venice Simplon-Orient-Express train played a significant role in the golden age of travel. The original train, the first Express d'Orient, left Paris for Vienna on June 5, 1883. Vienna remained the terminus until October 4, 1883. The train was officially renamed the Orient Express in 1891. The 1930s saw the Orient Express services at their most popular, with three parallel services running. The Orient Express, the Simplon-Orient-Express, and also the Arlberg Orient Express, which ran via Zurich and Innsbruck to Budapest, with sleeper cars running onward from there to Bucharest and Athens.

The 1920 vintage Art Deco cars in sparkling blue and gold take one's breath away. The journey between Paris and Istanbul is legendary and perfect for special occasions and celebrations like August and Lizzi's. They boarded the gleaming blue-and-gold carriages of the train at Paris Gare de l'Est midafternoon. August was dressed in a light gray tropical wool suit with light blue dress shirt and silver-and-blue tie, and Lizzi was in a white lightweight wool suit, straight skirt, and fitted jacket with high-heeled white sandals. Both were dressed to perfection. After being greeted by their personal steward and settling into their private cabin suite, they relaxed with a delightful afternoon tea.

Later, they enjoyed a delicious gourmet dinner in the opulent dining car, having an intimate conversation while trying to pick something very special from a beautifully appointed menu. A gold-and-blue crest topped the menu, and the selections were mouthwatering. August ordered a fine red Bordeaux and had it opened and decanted before they selected their main course.

First, August selected a lobster dish with sauce cardinale as appetizer, and then they both picked the filet mignon, sautéed wild mushrooms, and potatoes sarladaise. They skipped the soup so as to really enjoy the desserts offered from a dessert cart.

"This will take a while," said Lizzi, smiling. Her eyes caught the beautiful presentation of a whole torte sorrano. Nothing could be more fabulous! The base of this torte is layers of almond meringue with layers of praline cream, powdered sugar on top, and then topped with a stencil showing a *T*, which is dusted with cocoa. Voila! This is served with an espresso. Bon appétit!

"Amazing service," commented August while reaching for Lizzi's hand. They both had a good night's rest in their exquisite suite with gorgeous bedding and beautiful inlaid wood walls. It was very relaxing. The suite had impeccable service and attention to detail. It also had a fabulous interior of wood inlays, with engraved Lalique glass in the doors of the suites and also as dividers in the elegant club cars. It was a once-in-a-lifetime experience for August and Lizzi, a beautiful wedding gift from Lizzi's parents.

Next morning, they enjoyed the sublime scenery as the train travelled into Hungary and their continental breakfast was being served in their cabin suite. Lunch would again be taken in one of the opulent dining cars. For lunch, August wore a pair of white wool trousers with a dark blue silk shirt, and Lizzi came to the dining car in a stunning mint-green silk dress, tailored, with matching high-heeled pumps.

"You look absolutely stunning," said August to his new bride with a beautiful smile. It was a trip on an unforgettable special train for August and Lizzi that they would always cherish and remember.

These daydreams bring Lizzi so far into the past. Lizzi fondly remembers the trips she and August would take by car into wine countries, like the Mosel River valley, the Main River valley, into the Burgundy region of France, and into the Champagne vineyards in Epernay. The Mosel vineyards produce the finest Rieslings in Germany, and the Burgundy vineyards, as do the Rhône Valley vineyards, produce the very best of red and white wines, the ultimate essence of wines accompanying fine foods.

After August and Lizzi tasted these fine wines and purchased a variety of these wonderful wines for August's cellar, they drove north to Epernay to taste the very best in champagne and bring some home. While there, they also wanted to experience again the food the French prepared and presented with the ultimate flair.

Since it was time for dinner and it had been a long day of driving already, they stopped at a restaurant in Epernay. Inside, it looked like walking into a wine cave. After they were seated, the waiter came over to take their order. They started this experience with a bottle of Dom Pérignon accompanied by a wonderful salad. Oh, it was so nice to relax after a day of driving and wine tasting.

Lizzi looked so radiant and pretty in her white silk fine-pleated skirt and blouse coordinated together with a narrow golden leather belt. White high-heeled leather sandals finished her attire. She wore her pearl earrings and no other jewelry. August wore pearl-gray tropical wool trousers and a beautiful pale blue silk shirt open at the throat. Champagne flutes and salad plates were cleared.

And now, for the pièce de résistance, August ordered for Lizzi and for himself. He said to the waiter, "Tournedos of beef medium well for my wife and for myself please. Garçon, also please bring us a fine aged Châteauneuf-du-Pape to accompany this excellent dish."

August had a smile of anticipation on his face, thinking already of not only the tenderloin but also of this heavenly sauce. Looking over at his Lizzi, she was smiling too, thinking if the sauce would be as good or better than hers. August took her hand and squeezed it, most likely thinking the same. Lizzi was able to make that beautiful reduction sauce, and on a large fine china plate, it looked dark brown and shiny topped with chestnuts fried in butter and crunchy—a symphony! As they were talking and making their plans for the next few days, the wine steward came to the table with two bottles.

"Monsieur, s'il vous plaît, may I give you a choice of the finest of red wines before you take the Châteauneuf-du-Pape?" He held up in his hand carefully, like cradling a baby, a bottle of Romanée-Conti 1912!

"Well," August uttered with a smile, eyes in disbelief, "since you have this fine bottle in your cellar and are offering it to me, how can I resist?"

This was truly the best of the best. Only a few cases were made each year. Vines growing on a very small vineyard were pampered and well cared for as vines and in the winery. "This will be a memorable evening for us, my lovely Lizzi!"

August and Lizzi left the restaurant happy and satisfied, and as they got to their car, August opened his attaché case. Elated, he told Lizzi, "Look, my love, two more of the Romanée-Conti wines—a little younger, from 1920, but also great!" The wine steward realized that August knew his wines (at least the Burgundies and Rhône wines) and sold him two more bottles. The next morning, they decided to stop one more time at the Moët & Chandon winery, where they produce, in certain years, the great Dom Pérignon champagne. After seeing the seven-mile caves under the city, they had a little taste of this beautiful bubbly; and on their way through the large foyer with all the displays of their champagne, August purchased a case of the Dom Pérignon 1920 to be sent to their home.

As they left Epernay and therefore France, all their fond memories went with them. They took the route through Luxembourg and in to the Mosel wine region. Driving along the Mosel River, the scenery was breathtaking. On both sides of that river, all the way up the hills, were vines so beautiful to see, thinking what fine wine they were producing in this region too. August asked Lizzi, "Do you want to stop just to buy the wine, or would you enjoy a meal here in Germany?"

Lizzi was ready to get home and answered, "Just the wine, August. By lunchtime, we could be home, and I will make a wonderful meal to go with a bottle of Dom Pérignon, if you have another in your wine cellar. Maybe we can be outside on the terrace to have our lunch?"

August gave his Lizzi a kiss on the cheek, and they made one more stop to purchase their future wine. After all, that was the reason for the trip. Next stop: Darmstadt.

*   *   *   *

In the meantime, the lives of Frieda, Katja, and Lizzi have brought so much pleasure and happiness, but also much pain, sadness, and heartbreak. Lizzi's life in the twenties and thirties was the life with her wonderful husband, August, their three beautiful children, and a great and loyal governess, Mrs. Kramer, who adored her three children. She was not just the caregiver for them but she was also teacher and disciplinarian and stayed with Lizzi and August long after the children were grown to young adults.

Daydreaming is all right, but thinking of the present is also joy. Lizzi was awaiting her first child, and she was delighted about it.

When Lizzi and August's little boy was born, Lizzi's doctor recommended Mrs. Kramer to Lizzi. "She is a single lady who travelled and worked as a governess in many different places but now is available here. This would be where she wanted to be and settle down," Lizzi's doctor told her. Mrs. Kramer and Lizzi met during an interview, and they liked each other, and Mrs. Kramer moved into the house and made the Mansard her home with three rooms beautifully furnished. Mrs. Kramer was an interesting woman with an interesting life; she worked and travelled a lot to foreign countries. She had a lot of stories for the children as they got older. Lizzi was elated about her little boy, an image, a smaller version of August.

Lizzi now has to curtail her travels with August so she can have her little baby boy with her out in the beautiful rose garden when it gets a little warmer. When August comes home, he always showers Lizzi with gifts. Beautiful gifts like purses of crocodile leather, and not just brown or black but also in gorgeous colors—in dark green, light gray, or cognac. August had them packed in the store in very nice lacquer boxes. This time, it did not come in a lacquer box. It was a large flat box with a big bow on the outside. August found Lizzi in the kitchen with Mrs. Nietsche preparing the dinner for this evening, when Lizzi was expecting August to be home.

He put his arms around Lizzi and pulled her toward him tightly and said, "My sweet Lizzi, would you follow me? I want to show you something very pretty." Lizzi followed, thinking that August most likely bought her something "pretty" during his trip. As they entered the living room, Lizzi could see that big box but could not think of something that would fit inside.

She loosened the ribbon and opened the box and, sneaking her hand under the lid, said, "Oh!" She pulled out her hand and said, "What a most beautiful, soft, and cuddly coat!" She cried out, "Oh, how wonderful, my darling August!" Lizzi put the coat on and showed it off to August. "This is the most beautiful black, shiny mink coat I have ever seen!"

The style of the coat was stunning, full in the back and full sleeves with a little cuff. The lining was black silk with embroidery around the hem, and on the little pocket in the lining was Lizzi's embroidered name.

"Lizzi, you look absolutely breathtaking," August said to her as he pulled her close to him and kissed her. Last year, August bought her two silver foxes to wear with her light gray suit. Now that looked stunning!

*   *   *   *

The years went by fast, and Lizzi welcomed her second baby, a precious little girl: Frederika (called Friedl). She also had black hair and blue eyes. How lucky Lizzi was to have two beautiful children. Wolfgang, her little boy child, was growing up so fast, always playing with airplanes and wanting to be a pilot someday. How fast they grew up.

But now she had another little baby, and Lizzi adored her. After three months though, Lizzi noticed that Friedl avoided looking to one side, and her little face would never turn to the opposite side, and her chin stayed tucked into her shoulder. Lizzi, very concerned, took her baby girl to the same specialist who delivered the baby.

After the examination, the doctor explained to Lizzi, "Friedl was injured during the difficult birth. One side of the baby's face will not develop the same as the other side, and her head will stay in the position the baby is holding it now."

Lizzi was devastated by that news. Her beautiful daughter's face would only develop on one side. "No, this won't do!" she told the doctor. What can be done for her precious child?

After a conference with several specialists, Lizzi's doctor told her that they could perform a surgery to correct this injury. It was the right moment to perform this surgery now and not wait any longer. He would get the team together who would perform the surgery.

Lizzi went home with her little one to tell August and to prepare. Mrs. Kramer would take good care of her little boy. But her August saw it differently. "It is too risky to take a chance on *my* little girl's life or to put this fragile baby through this surgery."

Lizzi, on the other hand, wanted her beautiful little girl child to have a good and happy life. She packed and prepared to take this big step. When she was ready to leave, she looked if August was ready too. He confronted her once more and told her, "If you are determined to have this done and something will happen to *my* baby daughter, *you* need not come home." That was such a brutal remark, and the scary thing was August was serious.

With hurt feelings and feelings of abandonment, Lizzi then called a limousine and took her baby to the hospital. She had a bed in Friedl's room and stayed there. The surgery went well, and after two weeks, Lizzi, with her precious baby, went home.

She was welcomed with flowers throughout the house and met with open arms by her loving August. The only evidence of this very serious and complicated surgery was the incision on the side of the baby's neck, behind the ear. A beautiful future was ahead for Friedl, thanks to a loving and determined mother.

"There should be the christening for this precious little girl child, but not just yet," Lizzi told August. "She, little Frederika, needs some tender loving care first before we all can get together. She needs a lot of attention, just her," Lizzi added.

August understood his Lizzi and agreed.

August—either from a guilty conscience for not supporting his beloved Lizzi or from gratitude for giving him another beautiful child—showered Lizzi with gifts. The following Christmas, he ordered a special piece of sterling silver designed by the Silversmith. It was a most delicate and exquisite bowl. Lizzi cherished this piece given to her by August, thinking out of love. Many years later, Friedl chose to make it her dearest belonging, remembering August and Lizzi, her dearest parents.

* * * *

The sterling silver bowl August had made for Lizzi

On beautiful sunny days in May, Lizzi enjoyed her retreat in the garden by the fountain, holding her precious daughter, while her little boy was playing nearby. She was very content and happy just sitting there and admiring her two gifts from God. Her firstborn, her son, looked so much like his father. It made her think again of August, first seeing her love at the dance in the castle. How she felt when he held her in his arms while dancing and when his lips would come close to her face, dancing close, she had goose bumps running up her spine, and her heart would beat faster. Goodbye was always painful, and she felt that the evenings were far too short and the weeks to the next dance were far too long.

After some time, anticipating the next dance, little notes arrived for Lizzi, a date to meet and an itinerary of what he had planned, wanting to know if that would suit or please Lizzi. Since she already had fallen in love with August, Lizzi wanted him now to meet her parents and maybe come to her home more often to take walks in the beautiful forest and share a dinner with her family. It did not take many walks and dinners, and August fell in love with her—how beautiful life can be. A tender touch on her shoulder awoke Lizzi, and the handsome man from her dream was standing there, ready to put his arms around her and kiss her. She held on to his arm, and they entered the house.

They needed to talk about and plan a birthday party for their firstborn little boy, the one who wanted to grow up too fast. "How would it be if we had Wolfgang's school class in for birthday cake and games?" August smiled while sitting in his library, little Friedl on his lap.

"Maybe a puppet show to keep twelve boys focused and occupied?"

Mrs. Kramer was also present, and she agreed. She will engage the people who would perform shows in homes for children. Maybe even a magic act will do. After all, what child would not be intrigued and fascinated by magic? Lizzi sat with her loving August for a while, discussing the place where this all should be held. It is still a little too cool to be out on the terrace or in the garden for these little people, so it will be in the foyer by the wide curved stairway where the grand piano takes center stage. There is plenty of room for setting up the entertainment, and they put small garden tables and chairs for twelve little boys to be comfortable all afternoon.

August kissed Lizzi with a look of admiration in his eyes, knowing well that she would organize everything to perfection. August gave Friedl to Mrs. Kramer and went upstairs to get ready for dinner. As August was going upstairs, he was wondering what the surprise would be tonight: the dinner, the dessert, or the beauty of her table setting? Mrs. Nietsche was already busy in the kitchen as Lizzi entered. For Lizzi, it was an extension of culinary school. Every day, she could try something new and had a more than willing audience to taste, to eat with joy—her August.

Lizzi had followed August but stopped at the mailbox first to get the mail and saw she had a letter from her sister Frieda. As she read it, she called to August, "This is going to be an exciting time, this is an invitation to the christening festivities for Frieda and Christopher's little boy, Lukas. You and I are going to Calau. This will be such a wonderful reason to visit Frieda." Lizzi was happy that both sides of their families were invited, and hopefully, her sister, Katja, with her Philip, will also come. These festivities are as grand and important as a wedding, and Lizzi was looking forward to it.

Frieda and Christopher were living in a beautiful estate built in the 1600s, and the house was breathtaking. A big double door with hand-forged ironwork is the entry to a large, two-story-high foyer. On the back wall hung a beautiful tapestry, a Gobelin made in France as large as the wall showing the coat of arms of the Von Walde family. The floor in the foyer had large Italian flagstone, covered with several large silk carpets imported from then Persia. The very large great room, next to the foyer, was very inviting with the walls surrounded by built-in book cabinets, with handblown glass doors to keep safe a great collection of all leather-bound old books. There were plenty of comfortable chairs, with carved frames of ebony wood, covered in silver blue silk damask around an ebony table. This great room was two stories high with a Venetian chandelier hanging down.

One could spend an afternoon and evening there reading or enjoying coffee and Frieda's delicious desserts and conversation.

Over by a large stained-glass window was a beautiful big round ebony dining table with carved ebony chairs, also covered in that elegant silver blue satin damask for more formal use. Another stunning piece of art would await you as you turned the corner to go upstairs to the bed and bathrooms on the upstairs landing. Again, the size of the wall hung a painting, not a fresco on the wall, but a painting, framed in a gold leave frame, painted by a well-known German painter. One would have the feeling to be walking right up to life-size horses and riders in their black riding bridges and red jackets coming down a path out of the forest, so very striking!

The day came, and August and his Lizzi started their journey to Calau. It was an exciting time, and the train ride to Berlin was very pleasant, looking out at the scenery and having a lively conversation about the upcoming visit with Frieda and seeing her new baby boy. August with his Lizzi spent some time in the grand dining car having a delicious lunch of a delectable golden cheese soufflé and tender white asparagus. Both savored a very nice white Burgundy with it. They had to change trains at the Berlin station, and the train ride to Calau was not as long but gave August and Lizzi a chance to take a little nap.

A horse-drawn carriage awaited August and Lizzi at the Calau station to take them to Christopher and Frieda's estate. Christopher's driver, Franz, a very courteous gentleman, got Lizzi and August's luggage and helped them into the carriage, and they went on their way, through a dense forest, beautiful scenery, by an idyllic lake with wild geese enjoying the clear, clean water.

As they came out of the forest, they saw all the poppy fields stretching out on both sides of the road, the beautiful red poppies blowing gently in the breeze. Lizzi commented, "I never would get tired of this journey from Calau to Christopher's estate no matter how often I would make this trip. It always is beautiful and cool, due to the dense forest in the summer, and with a crisp white blanket of snow, it always is romantic in the winter." As they pulled up by the estate and entered through the gate, Lizzi and August saw Christopher and Frieda awaiting them with open arms.

Katja and Philip arrived two days later, and the sisters had a warm and wonderful visit before Sunday arrived, the day of Lukas's christening. He was a beautiful little boy child dressed in a white cotton batiste christening gown.

During the festivities, the three sisters had the opportunity to talk and sit together, bringing everyone up on their life's journey. These last few days were very precious to them but had to come to an end. In reality, parting was always touching.

On their way back on the train ride, August and Lizzi talked of having the christening for Frederika soon. They made their plans while on the train, and when they arrived home, they discussed it with Mrs. Kramer and Mrs. Nietsche. Since Friedl was a little older now and no longer an infant, it was decided that August would hold her on his lap during the ceremony.

Friedl was so pretty with her black hair and blue eyes, dressed in a white cotton batiste gown with short bodice, empire waist, with a pink ribbon and bow around it and little fine pleats down the front of the skirt. Little white stockings and white patent leather shoes completed the ensemble. She looked absolutely lovely, and August was proud to hold *his* little lady on his lap. Christopher with Frieda and Katja with Philip arrived for the ceremony and stayed another day. The festivities were like a wedding. Flowers decorated the house. The floral decoration on the table was breathtaking, white with deep pink orchids in a beautiful Lalique bowl. The dinner was superb.

"Let us taste and enjoy this light and crisp Riesling from the Mosel Valley with our first course of seafood," August announced. The first course was tiger shrimp in a lobster sauce with little toasted rounds of brioche bread with a bit of butter and Russian caviar. The main course was delectable. Everyone commented on the exquisite taste. Displayed on large Meissen china plates were beautiful veal tenderloins in a calvados sauce. On the side were caramelized apples and caramelized onions and saffron rice. For this meal, August had opened a beautiful Gevrey-Chambertin from the Côte d'Or

Burgundy region. As August was swirling this wine in his glass, he said with an admiring glance, "Exquisite!"

For the third course, Mrs. Nietsche brought in a large platter with an assortment of wonderful French triple-cream cheeses. To accompany this delicacy, August had brought up from his cellar a bottle of Château d'Yquem, a most beautiful of the finest Sauterne wines from the Gironde region. As if there was still room in the guests' tummies, Lizzi brought in her chocolate gâteau still warm, and it smelled heavenly. The guests had a choice of French roast coffee or another glass of August's beautiful Sauterne. The conversation around the table was lively and lasted hours. August and Lizzi along with her sisters and their husbands had an emotional bond. Happiness!

After dinner, the gentlemen went to August's library for conversation and good scotch, and the ladies sat in the living room with espresso, conversation, and Katja's diamond-shaped chocolate cookies while Mrs. Nietsche cleaned up. It was a wonderful celebration for a wonderful little girl, Frederika.

Time seemed to move so very quickly for everyone, and visits are not too often, although Katja and Lizzi have had more chances to visit, since they live so close together, only one hour by car. The three sisters though tried to have several visits in a year to get the children together. That seemed to be very important to them. In later years, the children would visit each other in the summer, especially after Lizzi's third child, Ilona, was old enough to travel by herself to Calau to visit Frieda (and their horses) every summer vacation, even during the war years. As she was getting older, she had a lot in common with her Uncle Christopher and the horses.

On a beautiful day, the last day of May, Lizzi was sitting by the fountain and Wolfgang and Friedl were playing nearby. Mrs. Kramer was reading to the children, but Wolfgang was not paying much attention. He wanted to play with his little airplanes. He decided he wanted to become a pilot and fly to faraway places. Lizzi's little boy was growing up too fast. Was he ever a little baby or a little boy? She missed that so for him.

Toward evening hours, Lizzi felt very tired and not too well, so she told Mrs. Kramer she would go in and lie down before dinner. That night, August feared for his beloved Lizzi, called an ambulance, and brought her to the hospital. After several tests and her physician conferring with other doctors, it was determined that Lizzi's pregnancy would not go full-term, and they would stand by for a premature birth. It was only the end of Lizzi's sixth month. On the second of June, Lizzi gave birth to a tiny two-and-a-half-pound baby girl. Lizzi and August did a lot of praying for their little one, in a makeshift incubator, with wonderful nurses, sisters, standing by day and night, dedicated to the welfare of that baby and the mother. After three months, in mid-September, August and Lizzi brought their precious baby girl home. This time, there would be a beautiful christening ceremony again with all three sisters and families being *one*. The name of this addition to August and Lizzi's family was Ilona, the middle name of Lizzi. Lizzi kept remembering the words of her physician, "If your precious baby stays alive and grows up, she will be a miracle."

The day for the christening was set, and invitations were sent. The house was decorated with white and pink baby roses and the Asian flowerpots along the walkway to the house displayed white and pink balloons. The first guests to arrive were Katja and Philip, and lunch was served out on the terrace. August and Philip enjoyed a scotch, and the ladies, Katja and Lizzi, enjoyed a champagne cocktail before lunch.

Mrs. Nietsche served a pear and blue cheese quiche with a most tender baked crust and a pear and walnut salad. Happy conversation outside on a beautiful sunny day lasted until afternoon when Christopher and Frieda arrived by limousine from the airport. After they freshened up and relaxed from their journey, champagne and a still warm and fragrant chocolate gâteau freshly baked by Lizzi were served in the living room, and everyone was enjoying this get-together. Christening would be tomorrow, Sunday, when Ilona Elisabetha had her day, dressed in a white christening gown, embroidered with little pink rosebuds. The three sisters in the meantime loved being together again.

Lizzi after the difficult birth of Ilona felt good again, and with her little Friedl by her side and Ilona in her arms, sitting out in the beautiful garden, Lizzi looked happy and radiant. Wolfgang would be playing nearby, and August would often come out now too with a smile and pride on his handsome face. He adored and loved his Lizzi and the three beautiful children she had given him. He loved to take the car, pack little Friedl into the front seat, and take her to town shopping. Friedl loved it, and she also loved hats, hats with matching coats, or dresses with a matching bonnet.

August would be so very proud of *his* little lady when he would bring her home and carried her into the house. Friedl of course would love to show off her new gifts from her father. They were a very happy family, and time was fleeting. The babies were growing into beautiful young children.

Not too long ago, Lizzi was sitting on her favorite bench by the fountain and rose garden, cuddling her youngest, and now, Lizzi is sitting on the bench by herself or with her August, while Mrs. Kramer is keeping a watchful eye on all three children playing or listening to their governess, reading aloud to them. Lizzi is contemplating what surprise to make for supper tonight. Maybe the family could be outside on the terrace with candlelight on the table for atmosphere. It will be such a beautiful evening tonight. A pastete (a pastry pocket filled with ham, cheese, apple, and caramelized onions) all in a beautiful pastry dough baked golden and served warm with a fresh, tasty salad made of greens was served. August would enjoy this pastete, love it, Lizzi knew.

August asked Lizzi to follow him into his library so they could talk. After Lizzi entered, August asked Lizzi to sit on his lap, and he would talk about something that would not pertain to the children. Lizzi got seated, and August held her tied. "I think we should purchase a new car, what do you think of that, Lizzi?"

Lizzi, with excitement in her voice, said, "What kind of car and can I come with you to the dealer?"

"Of course, I want you to come. Mrs. Kramer can take very good care of the children, maybe take them on an outing too, and you and I will go to Frankfurt to Daimler-Benz and pick a new model for us."

Arriving in Frankfurt, they took a cab to Daimler-Benz, and when they arrived, a gentleman walked toward them, smiling, and said, "Good afternoon, Mr. Eckert. So nice to see you, and I have two models in mind ready to test-drive. Are you and your wife ready?" Lizzi figured out right away that August had already everything arranged, that is, her August wasted no time. After the test-drive in both cars, they decided on the first one. Lizzi liked both, but they always had a convertible, so she liked the first car they drove. It was very nice, dark green outside. The top and interior were a rich cognac color, different from the last one. "It will be ready to be picked up in a week, Mr. Eckert," the salesman told August. "Or would you prefer we deliver the car right at your home?"

August said, "We will come to Frankfurt, and after a celebratory evening, we will stay overnight, and the next day, we will drive the new car home." Lizzi thought that very romantic and agreed.

Now, years later, as their babies grew into toddlers and toddlers grew into little people, they would present more of a challenge. Wolfgang would love any food his father would love, and he mimicked his father word for word, not just that he liked the food but also repeated August's compliments and called his mother Lizzi since that was what Wolfgang heard from his father. Friedl was very obedient and ate what was on her plate, but if she did not quite like it, she would not accept a second helping.

Ilona made it more of a challenge. She was hard to please. In fact, she was not just critical. She would find an excuse not to eat any of it if she did not like the looks even at her young age. Conversation at the dinner table was kept light since the children took part around the dining table and were taught not to speak while eating or when the adults would speak. After dessert, the children went upstairs. Mrs. Kramer attended to their needs while August and Lizzi enjoyed a coffee, a cognac, and some more serious or more intimate conversation. Suddenly, Lizzi was thinking again of little Lukas's christening celebration. It seemed so long, long ago. Lukas was now almost as grown up as Lizzi's Wolfgang.

Frieda had different rules for table etiquette than Lizzi. Little Lukas was given his dinner first as a baby and later after his schoolwork. His dinner was served to him ahead of Christopher and Frieda, since they enjoyed dinners much later in the evening by candlelight and music, most of the nights, when they had no guests. It was sad to see Lukas as a young boy sitting by himself, although it was a very nice set table, having served his dinner. But he was used to it. He grew up with it and accepted it. He turned out to be a wonderful young man.

Katja, not having any children yet, would have her dinner early evening, while Philips's days were long, and he wanted very little to eat and preferred an intimate setting, a little snack with a good scotch, and his Katja sitting with him for conversation. That would likely not change when they would have a little one. They were three lovely sisters, married to three wonderful young men together building beautiful lives, families, and homes in the 1920s and 1930s. All came through the horrors and destruction of World War I to live and see again the destruction of their precious families in 1939, the beginning of World War II, the war of all wars, destruction beyond belief.

*　　*　　*　　*

August wanted to have a family vacation, taking his new car on the road. He thought it had been a while since he visited his good friend, also his deckhand, Peter (Peppi), and his beautiful sailing vessel down in the Alps on Starnberger See (Lake Starnberg). Lake Starnberg, located in the midst of the Alpine Mountains, is 22.5 square miles, 12.6 miles in length, and is a freshwater lake with depth of 419 feet, the second-largest lake in terms of water volume.

August's sailboat is a 12 Metre sloop, an absolutely beautiful sailing vessel, sleek, graceful, and racy. The designation on 12 Metre does not refer to any single measurement on the boat and is not referencing the vessel's overall length, but rather, it measures the sum of the components directed by the formula that governs design and construction parameters. Typically, boats in the 12 Metre class range from sixty-five to seventy-five feet in length overall; they are most often sloop-rigged with masts roughly eighty-five feet tall.

The name of August's sloop was *ANMUT* ("grace" or "elegance"). Sailing with her was very rewarding, the scenery from the water glorious, and one felt free and unrestrained while on the boat. August has never used her for racing, only for recreation. August with his Lizzi and the children would drive south and have a vacation for a few days on his boat and then do some more sightseeing by car, maybe Munich and the other gorgeous lake, the Lake Königssee (Kings Lake).

They arrived at Starnberg, located at the northern tip of the lake. August contacted the deckhand Peter (Peppi) to meet him the next day to discuss what he planned. The family stayed in a first-class hotel and after dinner went to their rooms to rest since the next day would be very busy but fun. They had a full day of sailing, enjoying the scenery and the food and drink they had packed by the hotel. The evening ended with a very tasty dinner, light but very satisfying. For the family, it was early to bed that day.

Breakfast time came the next morning, and the girls, especially Ilona, wanted to have another day of sailing. August, loving this encouragement, agreed and arranged with his deckhand another day out on the Lake Starnberg. Should they run out of time, they could always skip Munich. Lizzi of course wanted to have just one day in Munich to have the pleasure of shopping. She said, "Could we all just have one day of shopping in Munich before we drive home? Mrs. Kramer is also on vacation to visit her sister in the Black Forest and won't be back until the end of next week? Besides, our Wolfgang won't come home from school until that time, when they get a short vacation, please, my dearest?"

How could August resist. He put his arm around Lizzi as they walked toward the hotel lobby, gave her a kiss on the cheek, and said, "One day, won't extend our vacation that long, and we are having such a good time, yes, my lovely Lizzi." They had another beautiful day out on the water with a soft breeze blowing. There was enough wind to fly the spinnaker, and Ilona tried for the first time to be the second deckhand. She wanted to learn tacking.

Evening came, and the *ANMUT* was coming in the cove and into her slip. "What a glorious day!" Ilona said. They all agreed as they were leaving the gorgeous *ANMUT* behind.

August stayed behind for a while, to talk with Peppi, and after they secured the sloop, August followed his family to the car. "Peppi will take care of the boat, and we will try and come down to Starnberg more often now that our girls are old enough to enjoy this lake and *ANMUT*," commented August as he got into the car. As Lizzi sat down in the passenger seat, she leaned over, gave August a kiss, and said, "You know that I love you very much?" She smiled and thought too what a wonderful week this was so far and how lucky she was. The two girls were sitting in the back seat, and all were ready to drive to the next destination.

"Muenchen (Munich)," Friedl and Ilona shouted.

"Muenchen (Munich) it is," said August with a smile.

12 Metre Sloop, Drawing by Traci Cole

Deep in the Alpine mountains surrounded by snowy peaks lies the city of Munich—a great city with many attractions to see and wonderful shopping for Lizzi, August, Friedl, and Ilona. August reached their hotel and gave the car over to the valet. They won't need the car since everything they wanted was in walking distance to the pedestrian zone. Munich was a city in the state of Bavaria, and the people there never hurried or were in a rush. It was a city of the most beautiful churches and cathedrals of welcoming cafés and restaurants, Opera House and concert hall, and the most beautiful park, Nymphenburg. The ladies and August found the shops they were looking for and had their *day*!

Evening came, and at dinnertime, they went to the dining room in their five-star hotel. A beautiful dining room, rococo style, it was very ornate and stunning. Waiters in tails were awaiting the guests, and August with his family was seated. The headwaiter came to pour a glass of champagne for Lizzi and August and left the captain's wine list in front of August. Their dinner and dessert was to remember! August and Lizzi also enjoyed their wine. Friedl and Ilona were fascinated by the ritual of presenting, opening, and then decanting this fine, old, red Bordeaux. Before the family went to bed, they agreed to stay another day to see the sights.

In a very quaint tearoom near the Nymphenburg Park, they enjoyed their lunch. They ordered the same food on the menu. It sounded very light and delectable. "Let us try the pastete here, to see if they are as good as Mama makes them," Ilona announced. Little baskets made from puff pastry are filled with lobster in a cardinal sauce. White poached asparagus on the side with salt-free butter was sprinkled with a little lemon. It was a very delicate dish, but all enjoyed it. Everyone also took part in choosing something off the dessert cart. Since it was the right time of year, nothing can beat the strawberry tarts. Beautiful equal in size red berries were covered in a red glaze and served with whipped cream. August and Lizzi had some very aromatic dark coffee with their tarts.

After this lunch, they decided to walk around the park and see all the beautiful plantings, the man-made lake with a little chateau at the edge, which was called the Porzellan-Schlösschen (porcelain castle), which housed the famous Nymphenburg china. It was very interesting to see, since everyone in this family loved beautiful china. Outside in the lake were three swans, two white and one black swan. The afternoon came to an end and so did their adventure. They left and went back to their hotel for another memorable evening and a comfortable night. Next morning, they packed the car, Friedl and Ilona in the back seat and Lizzi in the front with her beloved August. With maybe a small detour, or a stop, their destination was Darmstadt.

* * * *

Nineteen forty brought not only despair, heartache, and sadness but also a wonderful gift to Katja. The war with Russia had started. Philip had to leave with the units slated to fight the Russians, and shortly after, Katja found out she was pregnant with her first child, already in her fifth month. By April, she gave birth to a little baby girl. It was such a beautiful gift from Philip, but he was not there to share this with her. Katja wanted to fulfill her Philip's dreams and to be busy, not to painfully remind herself that her beloved Philip is fighting in Russia and could not be there and share the wonders of raising a wonderful girl, Krimhilde.

Katja started the process of rebuilding their home, built in the 1500s, and to replace it with something extravagant, not just up-to-date but for the future. This is what Philip wanted, and the plans were already drawn up. Katja and her daughter moved into the guest suite over the bakery, and the destruction of the old began so the construction of the *new* could follow.

More than a year later, the house was finished. The back of the house was mostly glass. Windows, with the push of a button, would move downward and disappear into the wall of the basement. Living, dining, and master bedroom would look out to the beautiful meadow with old apple trees and a creek running through, the sound of the water very relaxing and peaceful. The front of the house would occupy the large kitchen, where Katja would do her baking and cooking, provided with a large oven and stove, a cozy corner with easy chairs for reading and a desk for writing and maybe napping by it a little or for Krimhilde to do her homework.

It was a beautiful house because the materials used were beautiful. Marble covered the floors throughout, with stunning oriental carpets for warmth and comfort. Draperies were made of a sheer silk in all rooms. The kitchen had dark green lacquer cabinets and a large French stove in dark green lacquer. Again, the floor was of white marble. A long table, made of a chopping blockwood top, was centered in the kitchen to be used for preparation of food and also was for informal dining. Katja's mind turned to Philip, thinking if he would also love this house. Or would he get to see it?

One late summer day, early fall, one of those cold, crisp afternoons, Lizzi was sitting in the garden by the fountain, the remnants of summer's last roses still on the branches. She sat on her favorite bench, legs folded up, and was wrapped in a fur throw. She drifted off, the somewhat warm rays of an early winter sun caressing her face. She dreamed of her wedding, walking up the walkway to the front door on a sea of white rose petals on the arm of her beloved August. She dreamed of her three wonderful children, especially Ilona. She really was a miracle for Lizzi and for August now that the danger of losing her was past.

How lucky she was to find Mrs. Kramer, who was doing such an outstanding job teaching and leading them into a respectful life. Lizzi was also very grateful to have all three children now enrolled in a very prestigious private school.

As the rays of the early winter sun disappeared, Lizzi woke and was thinking of starting dinner for her precious family. She went into the house, entered the kitchen, and brought out her favorite little recipe books, part of her final exam at the culinary institute. They held all her favorite recipes, one for savory and the other for sweets, all her beautiful and tasty desserts she had handwritten. She had them bound in beautiful linen and had the writing imprinted in gold.

Tonight, being a little colder, Lizzi would make rouladen. Hopefully, Mrs. Nietsche could get the veal to fill the rouladen with. This was one of August's favorite dinners. Accompanying the rouladen would be wild mushrooms. This time of the year, Lizzi could get fresh chanterelles, fried golden in butter. A well-aged red Burgundy or Rhône would complement their dinner. Yesterday afternoon, Lizzi made crème brûlée to serve that night for dessert. She would end this dinner and this beautiful day with an espresso and her beloved August by her side.

Lizzi's decoration on the table were still some white roses she had picked that morning together with the deep blue hydrangea she was storing carefully for winter arrangements. A deep blue satin ribbon long enough to drape around each plate will complete the table. On August's large desk in the library, Lizzi prepared a section to serve dessert and espresso. Three small white rosebuds were adorned with deep blue ribbon by each place setting. Dark blue candles in tall candlesticks were on the desk for romantic lighting. Lizzi was ready to call for dinner.

The weather did change, and there were no more white roses, and the garden bench would not be occupied for a while. Lizzi is using now her window bench in their bedroom, overlooking the garden and the fountain with her bench. Lizzi is catching up on her correspondence with her two sisters. This lovely window bench is also a nice spot for catching up with reading and sometimes daydreaming. How fast the years go by. Her children are now young adults, completing their education very soon.

Wolfgang went to a flying academy to learn to fly, but he also attended regular schooling with the regular curriculum taught by academic professors. What Wolfgang was most excited about though was learning to fly gliders. He finished both and graduated in 1939 and entered the German Luftwaffe (German Air Force) the beginning of World War II.

Lukas, Frieda and Christopher's only son, studied to be a veterinarian and learned from his father breeding and raising horses. Lukas entered the war and joined General Rommel's Afrika Korps.

*   *   *   *

It was now late summer of 1939 when Lizzi's family planned one more outing by car to their favorite lake. Rumors heard already told them that the war was in evidence and not too far away. Lizzi and the children wanted to have one more outing to that most beautiful lake August called Florida. They did not know where that name came from, but the children liked it, and all referred to it that way.

Friedl and Ilona volunteered to go and see if they could find a gas station still open with gas available. They were two young, pretty girls who should be lucky, and they did find some. They came home with gas in the can, and the car still had enough in the tank to get them to Florida and home again. The car was all packed with food, drink, towels, a ball, and a blanket, and August, Lizzi, Friedl, Ilona, and Mrs. Kramer were on their way. Wolfgang was already missing in the family. He was at a military school and flying academy in Sonthofen, located in a beautiful part of the Alps. He did grow up to become a pilot. He was not to "fly far away," as Wolfgang put it years ago, most likely to fly for the upcoming war.

The late summer afternoon with family fun, sunshine, and good food did not turn out that way. A heavy cloud was hanging over August and Lizzi as they listened to the radio and heard Hitler declaring *war* on Poland. As they were driving home, the radio already announced that the German Wehrmacht (Armed Forces) was marching into Poland. When August, Lizzi, and their precious girls came home, they found in their mailbox the notice "From the Armed Forces" to get the car ready to have it picked up in the coming week. *With our Compliments to Hitler,* thought Lizzi. The nicest cars were confiscated to become "staff" cars.

Thinking back to happier times, Lizzi had clear memories of summer holidays she, Mrs. Kramer, Friedl, and Ilona spent on the North Sea, in the island of Rügen. They would play by the beach in the warm sun all day or go out on the hotel's boat, lying on the deck and taking in the warm sun. In the evenings after dinner, they would retreat to their rooms to enjoy the evening hours.

The sea breezes would gently move the curtains while they were sitting by the window, the children daydreaming and listening to Lizzi reading aloud great and wonderful stories by the Grimms and by Dickens and in later years books by Guy de Maupassant or poems by Goethe. Friedl and Ilona loved Goethe's drama "The Artist's Apotheosis," and Friedl was able to recite Goethe's song from the play "The Fisherwoman." They, Friedl and Ilona, both loved Guy de Maupassant's story "The Diamond Necklace." Those summer days fleeted by quickly, and soon it was time to get back home and to school. But the memories definitely lingered for the rest of the summer.

Lizzi and August's youngest, Ilona, was studying hard, taking International Law and Commerce at a private university. She really did not like English and would rather keep French as her favorite language, but her father, August, told her that English is important to her studies and also is the world's language, and if she liked French that much, she would have to take it as a second subject. It was difficult to learn two languages at the same time, so after the first two years, Ilona dropped French and studied hard to master English. All the International Law books were printed in English.

She also wanted to spend her time with more riding to master her jumping skills. She was a superb rider and jumper, and August was thinking that his youngest daughter was now ready to own another Trakehner, a European warmblood horse of East Prussian origin. The main stud farm, established 1731, and running until 1944, when the fighting of WWII led to the annexing of East Prussia by Russia, the town Trakehnen was then renamed Yasnaya Polyana. That breed of horse is superb in jumping, intelligence, and grace. August, her father, wanted her training to be rigorous, and she spent many hours of practice per week at the Marstall, a military facility with stables at the military garrison in Darmstadt. August had discussed this with Lizzi, and they agreed but kept it from Ilona.

August took a train to Stettin, where the Trakehner stud farm was then relocated due to the war with Russia. He purchased the horse for Ilona and accompanied the train that housed the horse

Maximilian for the duration of the trip to Darmstadt. The horse would again be stabled at the garrison's stables, and Ilona could have the same groom for her new horse and the same trainer. August had privileges there due to his connection to the cavalry and the grand duke.

On August's arrival at home, he entered the house and called to Ilona, "Sweetheart, I have a dance partner for you. Would you like to come with me to the Marstall, and I will introduce you to him? His name is Maximilian, but you may call him Maxi, and he will respond." Curious, Ilona came down the stairs, smiled, and with a questioning look at her father thought, *Marstall, could it be?* Without saying anything, she picked up her boots in the little tack room inside the garage and came out smiling. They together went by streetcar to the Marstall, and August presented Maxi to his daughter.

Breathless, elated, and with tear-covered cheeks, Ilona ran to her Beautiful Maxi, black with four white stockings, and put her arms around him. "He is mine, really mine?" Her father hugged her and said yes. Ilona got to stay long enough to pet and kiss and ride Maxi, and it was time to get home for dinner.

Ilona's horse, Maxi

Ilona's trainer found her to be the right subject for training to become a skilled jumper to qualify for the 1948 Olympic Games. Ilona would be twenty-one years of age then. Although she was too young to enter the equestrian team for Germany, but with her training of over fifteen years, she definitely would qualify at that age. However, this all was not to be. World War II was going on, and it was brutal. A lot of cities were already destroyed, and millions of people, military, and civilians vanished. Hitler was never going to surrender.

The first to be called and to be killed was August and Lizzi's most precious boy, Wolfgang, their only son. A pilot of a Stuka, a dive bomber flying a mission over Poland, their air defense hit Wolfgang's plane, but he made it back to his air base in Dessau-Rosslau and there burst into flames and crashed on the airfield. The two officers, who came to August and Lizzi's home bringing this bad news, were sure that Wolfgang did not use his parachute because his gunner was gravely wounded and could therefore not jump.

Lizzi's August was called to service next but due to his age was not called to combat but served on the staff in Berlin.

The third young man called was Christopher and Frieda's only son, Lukas, who went to Africa to serve in a tank division with the "Desert Fox" General Rommel and gave his life at El Alamein.

The fourth man called was Katja's Philip, who gave his life at the siege of Stalingrad, the most devastating and the longest battle, with unbelievable losses of lives on both sides. Katja though believed her Philip to be alive and would come back to her. She had a little baby girl Philip would never have the pleasure and pride of knowing. Krimhilde would never meet her beloved father. Katja waited until her death in 2002, always strongly envisioning her Philip walking in the door any day. Philip did not return.

The Battle of Stalingrad, so very costly on both sides, started September 1942 and lasted until 1943. The German commander of the Sixth Army, General Paulus, assisted by the Fourth Panzer Army, advanced on the city of Stalingrad. His primary task was to secure the oil fields in the Caucasus, and to do this, Paulus was ordered by Hitler to take Stalingrad. His final target was to take Bakus. Joseph Stalin, this city named after him, for simple reasons of morale, could not let the city of Stalingrad fall. Stalin's order was, *"Not a step backwards."* Statistics show how brutal this battle was on both sides for this so very important city.

German Army: Led by General Paulus	Russian Army: Led by Marshal Zhukov
1,011,500 men	1,000,500 men
10,290 artillery guns	13,541 artillery guns
675 tanks	894 tanks
1,216 planes	1,115 planes

Marshal Zhukov, with the help of the Twenty-Fourth, Sixty-Fourth, Fifty-Seventh, and 521st Armies, surrounded the city of Stalingrad. General Paulus could have broken out of this trap in the first stages of Zhukov's attack but was forbidden from doing so by Hitler.

A message came out before the airfield was taken. The message by a German officer said, "No, we are not going to be captured. When Stalingrad falls, you will hear and read about it. Then you will know that we shall not return."

Africa with General Rommel was a battlefield from June 1940 to 1943 and ended with the defeat of the German tank battalion.

May 1940 was the invasion of France, and Hitler defeated France by June 1940.

June 22, 1941, was Hitler's invasion of Russia. The operation was called Barbarossa. Hitler's ideological aims to conquer the western Soviet Union were to populate the region with Germans and use Slavs as a slave labor force for the Axis war efforts and to seize the oil reserves of the Caucasus. But Hitler failed, splintering the German army into three fronts.

In six years of war, so many families and their homes and so many brave soldiers on three fronts were lost and destroyed. It was a devastating war that Hitler unleashed and had no intention of stopping because he had no vision, only greed and hunger for power.

How good, peaceful, and enjoyable the years had been for Lizzi and August with their precious children before that terrible war. She could then dream of all the joyful days and years by the fountain and her beautiful rose garden—in the summertime, the suppers on the terrace, sitting until dusk, until the children had to go to bed, and in later years, doing their homework and then just Lizzi with her August enjoying a glass of wine or champagne, listening to the fountain and cuddling together.

Life was then tranquil and satisfying. Excitement then was still a part of their lives, especially starting the opera season in October with the grand opening of the season, when the grand duke and duchess took part in opening night. Lizzi and August in formal attire would be picked up by limousine, and then Mrs. Kramer and the girls were allowed to stay up longer, playing piano, and Friedl and Ilona would dance. Sometimes, Frieda and Christopher would come from Calau to join Lizzi and August on opening night at the opera. They would stay a few days, and Lizzi's youngest, Ilona, would love it when they would come since they could talk again about horses.

Friedl was more the artist. She started to crochet and made beautiful dresses, coats, and blouses. She herself created the styles and for that style chose the right yarns. It was so amazing what she had learned in finishing school, but she also had the talent at her young age. Friedl was dreaming of someday having a whole room full of yarn.

Wolfgang, the eldest, was not so much dreaming. He was determined at a young age already to be a pilot as soon as he was old enough. Lizzi thought her children were growing up too fast.

Ilona was having such serious conversations with Christopher about breed of jumpers she liked, style of riding from the proper gear to clothes to proper helmet and boots to posture. She was fascinated with Christopher's knowledge and experience. In that time, Frieda and Lizzi retreated into the kitchen or were sitting in the library talking and reminiscing. By evening then, the result of their joint efforts was astounding and delicious, and the table looked as if they were expecting royalty.

Plans were for Ilona after her sixteenth birthday to travel by train to Calau to visit Frieda and Christopher. A few days into her visit, Frieda told Ilona, "I have a wonderful surprise for you, now that you are a young lady. We are taking the train to Berlin and staying for two or three nights in a grand hotel right off Kurfürstendamm where all the beautiful shops are. We also will take a bus to Potsdam, so you can see Sanssouci again, now that you are older and enjoy the history and culture." It sounded exciting to Ilona to make this trip with her wonderful aunt Frieda, but staying there at the estate would sound better, since the horses were there. Well, Ilona guessed, she is not as grown up as Frieda thinks. But Ilona was not going to say so, since Frieda was so happy to have planned that for her.

A little before noon, the train pulled into Berlin's main station, and a cab took the two ladies to their hotel, Kaiserhof, where they freshened up and went to the beautiful dining room to have lunch. They took their time to study their menu, and both were ready to order as the waiter approached. On a beautiful large white china plate with the crest in gold of this hotel on the rim, a golden brown vol-au-vent (puff pastry pockets) filled with shrimp in a lobster cream was placed in the center and on the side a mixture of raspberries and strawberries sprinkled with cognac.

Aunt Frieda had champagne, and they allowed Ilona a spritzer, a small amount of champagne in the bottom of the flute and filled with carbonated water. *So this is what it's all about when one grows up?* thought Ilona. After lunch, the two ladies started down Kurfürstendamm and entered a jewelry store. The owner came right toward Frieda and greeted her like this was all arranged. Frieda looked at Ilona and whispered, "Come, sweetheart, and look at these rings. Christopher and I wish to buy this for you, and you get to pick one of these." There was a most beautiful collection on this tray. Which one should she pick?

There was one that stood out right away—a gold band and on top of the band was gold filigree built up like an upside-down little basket, which held a beautiful little ruby. The jeweler approved with a nod, and Aunt Frieda had a satisfied smile on her beautiful face. She pulled Ilona close and hugged her. The rest was devoted to business, while Ilona admired her precious ring with tears in her eyes.

The rest of the afternoon was spent with a little shopping for Aunt Frieda, and Ilona was asked several times to give her opinion on items that Frieda was buying. Frieda, like Ilona's mother, Lizzi, had good taste, and Ilona's opinion always was positive. Frieda and Ilona stopped on the way back to the hotel in a lingerie shop, and after Aunt Frieda purchased a beautiful camisole for herself, she asked Ilona, "Would you like one also, for under a sheer summer blouse?" Before Ilona could answer, Frieda told the clerk to put another in Ilona's size in the package. Was this Christmas? It was a wonderful and lovely outing with Ilona's favorite aunt.

After a marvelous dinner and a good night's sleep, the two ladies took the bus to Sanssouci the next day. It was truly more beautiful than Ilona remembered. Sanssouci, the eighteenth century palace, the summer palace of Frederick the Great, king of Prussia, is in the rococo style and is smaller than its French baroque counterpart, Versailles. The royal gardens and fountains are magnificent and elegant. The palace is majestic enough to compete with the most iconic palaces in Europe. The stairs that surround the palace are incredible. It was for Frieda and Ilona a *one-time* experience although they did not know this at the time.

Early morning the next day, the two took the train home. During the train ride, they enjoyed in the dining car a tasty breakfast, and as the train pulled into the Calau station, they could see Christopher waiting with a big smile on his handsome face. For having reservations about Berlin, versus staying in Calau, Ilona was now almost ashamed for that thought she had for a moment. It was a wonderful memory Ilona would have in her heart for many years to come. That was priceless!

Travelling and visits between the sisters came to a stop now since the nightly bombings were too frequent, and it was not safe any longer to travel by train. Friedl's school, located in the Odenwald Forest, was pretty safe, and as long as the trains kept running, Lizzi, along with Ilona, would look forward to visiting Friedl, and they took their chances. Ilona especially would look forward to these weekends, since she missed her sister Friedl very much, and when they got there to their hotel, she became very anxious to get to the finishing school to see her beloved sister.

For Ilona, the house was so empty. Friedl was missing, and the only happiness were the weekends, looking forward to being with Friedl, sitting close to her, cuddling and listening to her stories. But the goodbyes were always very difficult and brought tears to both. Coming home, Ilona went to her room and sat on her window bench, crying. She was longing so for her beloved sister to come home. Ilona decided to write Friedl a letter since she would receive it before they would see her again.

> *I am so very, very lonely and so very frightened. It was so long ago that there was peace. The war is dragging on, and one cannot remember life without war! The bombings are accelerating, and our fear of "when will it be our turn" is getting stronger. We are living with the shrill sound of the sirens nightly now, standing outside on the street to observe where the bombers will be attacking this night, and we are very relieved when it is not our turn yet. A selfish thought, but oh so true. All my tests for the baccalaureate have to be taken in the air-raid shelter of the school, and I must ponder why and for what. Do we have a future? I miss you so dearly, your silent courage and your calmness. I am longing for the day you will return to me. Yours, Hugs and Kisses.*

In early May of 1944, Friedl graduated and returned home.

On one of the weekends, when August would come home, he brought with him several friends. Among this group was a lieutenant in the panzer corps (tank battalion). His name was Horst Schaffner, and he was very handsome, could play the piano, and could dance. After some more visits, he and Friedl got to know each other, and after a few more visits and going out on restricted dates due to time and curfew the war demanded, Horst proposed to Friedl. They of course waited to ask August if it would be allowed. August not only gave his blessing to Horst and his precious Friedl to marry but also gave the gold of his Pour le Mérite for two beautiful engraved wedding bands for the couple.

Lizzi then got very busy with plans for a wedding, which was rather difficult during this time. But Friedl was very much looking forward to her wedding the following spring on her birthday, March 2, 1945.

Lizzi was occupying her window bench, daydreaming. This horrific war was marching on, claiming so many lives. Lizzi had to sacrifice her only son, her precious boy child. Her heart was aching. She saw her Wolfgang. He was so very handsome in his uniform the day he left her and August. He was her beautiful first lieutenant, going off to war, finally flying his plane, so very young yet so grown up. She could imagine kissing him goodbye, so very painful, never to see him again.

She had startled herself with the kiss and woke up, coming back to reality. She left this bedroom looking for her August, who came home some weekends. She found him in his library, reading. She sat on his lap, and he put the book aside, put his arms around her, and kissed her. The weekend had passed, and it was time for August to get back to Berlin. How long would it be before he could come to her again?

*   *   *   *

The bombing raids became much more frequent, and Lizzi, her two daughters, Mrs. Kramer, and Mrs. Nietsche spent a lot of nights in the air-raid shelter, frightened that it might be "their turn" that night and relieved when it was over and all five could go back to their beds. It was September 11, 1944! The alarm went off, and Lizzi was thinking, *will it be our turn tonight?* They again rushed with their favorite things into the air-raid shelter.

The first planes dropped the lights. They called them Christmas trees. They would illuminate the sky and the city. This time, Lizzi's city was in daylight. The B-17 bombers followed, and everyone lying on the dirt floor in the shelter on their stomachs could feel the ground swelling and rolling, a terrible feeling and so frightening when the first bombs hit their target. The sky was showing the waves of bombers coming from the west, north, and south, wave after wave for forty-five minutes though it felt like hours. The bombers dropped the incendiary bombs first, and the whole city started burning. Then they dropped the high-explosive bombs to destroy what was still standing.

The whole city, the core and the residential part, was destroyed. But no industrial factories were even hit. It was a *total* attack and very, very costly. In the end, it was calculated that twenty thousand people lost their lives and seventy thousand people were homeless. This old city, full of history, art, and beauty, lay in rubble and was burning for over a week. There were no ambulances, no fire trucks or firemen, no hospitals, as they were in ashes too.

Lizzi's August, on one of his last visits, had the family moved to his apartment building to be safe in an air-raid Shelter, rather than his house with only a cellar. Next to the apartment building where they would have their flat was a beautiful sandstone apartment building where August's twin brother, Arthur, and his wife, Lillie, were living. They also joined August's family in the shelter. August's brother, Arthur, was the state attorney general. His office was in Darmstadt, which was now too totally destroyed. Lillie was a wonderful aunt and came to visit quite often. Lizzi still had some tea and saved it for guests. She always had enough ingredients to make up some goodies to share with Lillie and enjoy her company.

Although the air-raid shelter was a good solution for the safety of August's family, it was, after all, not necessary, but a good precaution, not believing what the enemy was telling the Germans on leaflets, dropped on the area where August's home was located. The propaganda leaflets told the homeowners in the Villa Colony, a specific area with beautiful homes, that the Allied bombers would not bomb that area because it would be needed after the war for the American military families to live in. No one believed it. How would they know about these homes?

But after 1945 and the war's end, they found out it was correct. The same was true for General Eisenhower's headquarters. Instructions were given not to bomb the IG Farben Building, since this was to be Ike's headquarters during the occupation of Germany. Truly, after the war's end, no damage, not even artillery damage, was inflicted on the building, in the midst of destruction in Frankfurt.

After the cleanup in the destroyed city was progressing and most of the rubble covering sidewalks and streets was removed and thousands of people who were killed, many of them still in the cellars of apartment buildings inside the city, were disposed of, the city, once known for her beauty and art, was in ruins, empty, gray, and dead. August and Lizzi with their family loved this city of Darmstadt where they would make their home, a city where his father had lived, a city so very rich in history and culture.

"As spice of my life, I could not wish for better company than that which this city offered me—this place, which in any case would be one of those where I would pitch my tent forever, if fate had let me choose my place of residence of my own free will." These words, written by Hans-Colbert Hoffman in 1783, would still be valid for this city today had it not been destroyed by a war, a costly war that Hitler had started with no end in sight.

Now, Lizzi needed to get busy preparing for Friedl and Horst's wedding next March. The dress was her biggest worry. She had designed it, had the many yards of material, and now it was important that the gown be completed. There was to be a lot of handwork on the gown. It would be exquisite. It would have petals made of white silk, sewn together to form roses, and in the center of each rose was a pearl. This gorgeous lace handwork was then sewn over the white silk and made into a breathtaking gown. The veil of white silk organdy was studded with pearls. Her bridal flowers of white roses were formed into a Biedermeier bouquet.

The entry and foyer were decorated with white lilacs and white ribbons. The gown was completed, and the day came. It was March 2, and it was Lizzi's beautiful Frederika's birthday! It also was her wedding day. The groom arrived in full dress uniform.

They were a beautiful couple coming out of the makeshift Paulus Cathedral, the only church restored enough to be used. As Friedl and Horst came outside, walking together arm in arm, under an arch of raised swords, it was truly magnificent. The music and dancing was interrupted by midnight by an order for the lieutenant and his four companions to return to their unit, which was going back into action. Friedl frantically awaited word, some kind of word, some news about her beloved bridegroom.

*　*　*　*

There was still no news as of May 1945. And there were some tense days, deciding if to surrender or not to surrender. It was up to the city fathers, but there was very little left to die for. Most of the population already died during September 11, 1944, and the survivors had been relocated into the country with relatives or families volunteering to take some displaced families in.

The few people left were ready to surrender to the American tank battalion waiting at the entrance to what once was their city of Darmstadt. Everyone from this neighborhood was standing outside, behind the iron gate to the house. They watched, in fear for their lives, since all German people were told time and again: if they surrendered, they would all be killed. Only women and one older man were waiting, not knowing if this would be the day, the end of their lives. They all hung on to each other and prayed.

In the distance, they could hear the thunder of the tanks on the cobblestone streets after they entered their city, coming up Rhine Strasse and turning to Frankfurter Strasse. The tanks came into view, and on the front of each tank was a soldier sitting with machine gun in hand, watching every house, ready to use the machine gun or pull back if needed. General Eisenhower's motto was "If our tanks get any resistance, we will pull them back. The artillery will come in and wipe out what threatened us and we come back in to mop up."

There was no resistance in Darmstadt, and the tank battalion rolled through Darmstadt toward Frankfurt. Everyone sensed the danger and disappeared into their homes. Was this horrendous war really over, or was it only on hold? No one could believe it to be over. Lizzi had not heard anything from the German Armed Forces or from August. She was still hoping and waiting that he came through the terrible slaughter in and around Berlin by these barbarians, the Russians.

Occupation started, and the American troops started to come in, moving into the garrisons left by the German army and setting up their field hospital inside one of the beautiful parks. They had two soldiers at all times riding in jeeps, checking everyone on the street for ID. There was mandatory curfew, and the people could only be on the street from 0800 hours to sundown. It was now summer of 1945, and Friedl had not heard anything about her Horst either. The mood in the house was somber and sad. Not only did they not hear from August and Horst but there was also nothing, no news at all, from Frieda and Christopher, who were also overrun by these barbaric Russian armies.

It turned out to be shocking news. Christopher and Frieda's estate was destroyed. (These Mongolian hordes most likely used their beautiful horses for food.) Both dear Frieda and her wonderful Christopher were killed as they overran that area. They burned everything in their path and made it part of Russian territory.

Friedl joined the Red Cross to get some news now and then on the status of Horst and of August, her father. There was no news from Friedl's Horst, but much later, in 1949, Friedl got a letter from the Red Cross. One of Horst's superior officers had written this letter to the Red Cross describing that the four officers and their driver were called back from a wedding, and all were in the car coming back to the Western Front, but none of the officers—five of them with the driver—made it to their units. That would mean they were under artillery fire as they neared the front lines, and the car most likely was destroyed with the officers in it.

Friedl knew then that Horst would also not return. It was now "war six, our family nothing." By this date, Lizzi also had not heard from her beloved August. Since he was in Berlin and Frieda and Christopher were in Calau, not far from Berlin, and the Russians overran both places, Lizzi had to believe that maybe August had been killed too.

Lillie's husband, Arthur, August's twin brother, committed suicide, distraught over the outcome of that devastating war and the horrendous losses of his family. August's family sacrificed all their men. Like the rest of Germany, they lost two generations of men, young and healthy men, in WWII. Poor Lillie could not live with this loss either and had a terrible breakdown and spent five years in a clinic.

When she returned from the clinic, her brother, George, and sister, Anita, took her in. They lived together in a very pretty apartment, very elegant, with many antiques and art pieces to create a beautiful atmosphere. George had been an art dealer for many years and could most likely find anything one's heart desired. He was the youngest of the three siblings but died first in 1968. Lillie, a sweet lady who loved Friedl very much, died in 1978. Anita, the oldest of the three, died in 1982.

*   *   *   *

Lizzi, Friedl, Ilona, and Mrs. Nietsche started their lives slowly, trying to get used to the overwhelming changes since the end of war in 1945. It was hard to live in a place that was once a beautiful city, a treasure, and now there is nothing. After the September 11, 1944, bombing, Lizzi gave Mrs. Kramer a choice. "If you wish to leave and live with your sister in the Black Forest, this would be all right. The children are old enough now, and in a small village, it would be most likely safer for you." Mrs. Kramer took Lizzi's offer and contacted her sister and then moved there. Mrs. Nietsche, however, wanted to stay with Lizzi, and they agreed that she could stay as long as she wanted.

Friedl and Ilona would take their bikes and ride into the countryside to beg for food. They sometimes did not do well; but other times, they were lucky and had milk, potatoes, maybe bread, but rarely some butter. There were no stores since nothing was built up yet. Sometimes trucks would bring some food, fresh fruit, meat, and milk. Mrs. Nietsche would stand in line for these items; but sometimes, she returned empty-handed.

Katja and Krimhilde would visit Lizzi and bring some food. Or Friedl and Ilona would take their bikes and ride into the Odenwald, where Katja lived, to bring home some good things. Time marched on, and it sadly looked as if Lizzi, Katja, Krimhilde, Friedl, and Ilona were the only survivors left after this horrendous war. Only five women—no husbands, no boy children. They had to think that there was also no future.

When Katja would visit, the two sisters would sit together in the library and talk a while, and then Friedl or Ilona would hear them crying. It was heartbreaking! When Ilona completed her baccalaureate, she too pondered what it was for. *Is there a future? Is this ugly war really over, or is this war only taking a break?* Ilona was thinking. *What will I do with my education? Was it all for nothing? Will Germany ever be invited to the Olympic Games?* Then Ilona thought of dear Mama, Lizzi, and her dear sister, Friedl, and suddenly, she realized that she was just feeling sorry for herself, that both women were really hurting and lost almost everything. Ilona would go look for her sister and mother and give them a big kiss.

It was getting closer to Christmastime, which was always a very important time for Lizzi's family; but now, she was not sure what to do. Maybe they just could have some good fragrant greens, some candles, white cotton for snow, and a few decorations. But what about food? Well, that might be solved too, Lizzi hoped.

At least she still had her beautiful home. They had the grand piano, and the castle still had the chapel. It already sounded better than Lizzi thought to start with. Lizzi also knew, since Katja still had the bakery, that they could get some cookies from her loving sister. If it doesn't snow, Friedl and Ilona could bike to Katja's. Or Katja with Krimhilde, who were very lonely too, might want to come to Darmstadt to be with Lizzi, Mrs. Nietsche, and the girls. That sounded encouraging, and Lizzi left her little place on the window bench and came downstairs to get something together with Mrs. Nietsche that would suffice for dinner.

Lizzi always set a beautiful table, even now, when food was sparse. The table was very important. While Lizzi was in the kitchen foraging for dinner, Mrs. Nietsche set the table with beautiful china and silver service, got the candlesticks, and found some more candles. It was an inviting table, and all enjoyed the dinner. There was silence around the table, and to break the somber mood, Lizzi started talking about Christmas and her idea to see what Mrs. Nietsche, Friedl, and Ilona wanted. They all agreed to a little celebration to honor the Christ child's birthday, and it also would be good for the four women. It broke the ice, and everyone was making suggestions and eager to follow Lizzi's lead.

That evening, Lizzi sat by the window and wrote a note to Katja, inviting her and Krimhilde for Christmas. Advent came and went, and Christmas arrived at the door. The decorations looked very festive since Lizzi always had beautiful things to make Christmas special and lovely.

Katja and Krimhilde arrived with all kinds of food, especially wonderful cookies. Katja's specialty, always for Christmas, was a delicate and delicious treat, not necessarily a cookie: baking oblaten, made from egg whites and sugar, available at Christmas in Germany and Austria for convections, rectangle five by eight inches in size and very thin and fragile. Katja made chocolate ganache and layered it with oblaten, then placed it in the refrigerator to get it cool enough to slice into diamond shapes, about one inch in size. They were wonderful, tongue-melting morsels, served cold. Lizzi announced, "I am going to look into August's wine cellar and bring something very special to accompany our fine dinner, and just maybe, my precious August will come back to us."

Lizzi and Friedl both did not want to play any Christmas music, which was all right with everyone, but the conversation became lighter as the evening progressed. The heavy cloud that was hanging there before got a little lighter after they all returned from the Christmas service at the beautiful little chapel, and during the remainder of the evening, there were even some little smiles and prayers for the ones missing.

The next morning, which was Christmas morning, they all got together in their robes, and Katja made her famous hot chocolate: bring milk to boil, chop dark chocolate, and pour the hot milk over the chocolate, stirring rigorously. Katja also brought the breakfast pastry. She served the croissants, brioche, and some rolls with caramelized nuts and cardamom warmed from the oven along with cups of hot chocolate, a feast for kings.

Christmas afternoon was with tea and cookies. Lizzi was attempting to play the piano, and no one objected, so she played some Christmas music. It showed that even in times of grief, the nature of a human being is to find ways to ease the pain and, even if for but a second, to forget the longing and sadness and to steal a little bit of contentment. It worked for everyone that Christmas day.

Next day, when the parting came, faces were a little brighter than on the day when they arrived. But Lizzi was a little sad and even shed some tears when Katja and Krimhilde departed. They promised to come back on New Year and bring the dinner. Lizzi talked with Mrs. Nietsche, and the two women were going to find the makings for a croquembouche—little cream puffs with patisserie cream inside and built up into a Christmas tree. This was always Lizzi's masterpiece on the Christmas dessert table. But since Christmas is now over and if Lizzi finds what she needs, she just would make the cream puffs filled with patisserie cream. And she would serve them sitting on a bed of crème anglaise sauce on her beautiful Christmas dessert plates. This too would look beautiful and would taste delicious, and not as many cream puffs would be needed if she was not making the tree.

Lizzi also knew where she could find and get some coffee along with the other ingredients. She will have to pay a lot, but for this get-together, it would be worth it and would taste heavenly along with the cream puffs. Lizzi and Mrs. Nietsche went to see Mr. Fertig. Mr. Fertig had a delicatessen store and a seafood market in the city before the bombings but lost it all the night of September 11, 1944. Most likely though, he still had his contacts from before the bombing of Darmstadt. He told Lizzi, when they saw one another last, that if she was in need for anything, to please call or tell him, and he might be able to help. Lizzi had always been a very good customer, and he always could count on Lizzi to buy some of his "finds" (very expensive finds). But if it was something tasty, Lizzi would always purchase what Mr. Fertig had available.

The two ladies actually came home with a shopping bag. Mr. Fertig came through for Lizzi. That was wonderful news. Lizzi had cream, milk, flour, and even some cardamom seeds, nuts, and a little flask of vanilla extract. "This will do, since a vanilla bean is impossible to find. Coffee!" Lizzi called out. It had been a long time since there was coffee. Lizzi and Mrs. Nietsche looked so very happy and satisfied. Friedl and Ilona had not seen them like this for a long, long while.

Everyone was surprised and aware of the mood in the house and most likely felt a little guilt over being so happy, like this was not allowed. Suddenly, looking at each other, both Lizzi and Mrs. Nietsche started to cry. Maybe it was tears of joy because of the good things that suddenly appeared in this time of utter despair.

Lizzi gave her two darling girls a big kiss, saying, "There will be cream puffs, patisserie cream, and crème anglaise for New Year! I also found a wonderful aged sauterne in August's cellar." Maybe there is a great need for these four survivors and also Katja and Krimhilde to have a few celebratory hours on New Year's Eve. Maybe in the New Year there will be some, just a little, good news?

*   *   *   *

There was no good news in the beginning of 1946. Friedl desperately went every week to the Red Cross office. They had a makeshift office in the first floor of what once was a bank. It was no longer a building, just part of the walls still standing; the inside was all burned out and existed only of rubble. They had no news about Friedl's father or about Philip. They had to wait and keep hoping.

In the early months of winter 1946, the days and months went slow, but if Lizzi, Mrs. Nietsche and the girls stayed off the street, or only went out during the hours of the day, no one would get in trouble. Slowly, the city got a cleaner look. The rubble on the streets, especially on every corner where the inside of this apartment building was burned out and all cellars were cleaned out. It started to look already better. Construction companies from other cities came to start rebuilding, first on the ones with only partial destruction. They needed housing badly, or there will not be people living in this city, no housing, no stores, no banks, no medical facilities or churches and because of that, *no* people. They are still in the country and waiting to come back to their city.

After the Marshall Plan, American money got Germany revitalized, and the German people started to come alive. Businesses from other cities came in as soon as the buildings started to go up. Darmstadt needed it, for they lost so many people who worked and lived in the city and gave it life.

Since they started in a hurry to build so the people in the country could come back, they neglected to rebuild it as it was once in its glory. But this was now a new era with a new influx of people. The old just had to move over to make room for the new. If it were not for America, the Germans would not even be able to start building. The infusion of money was vital to the surviving few who had to carry the weight now alone.

So far, trucks with supplies of food, water, and essentials were coming through Darmstadt several times a week. After the basements of apartment buildings were cleaned of the dead and were secured to be safe, the water was turned back on again in the city, and Lizzi and the girls no longer had to carry the water from the gardens the city dwellers had outside the city little garden patches for planting flowers, vegetables, or just have a little garden house to escape the city in summer's heat. These gardens all had water, well water, and it was safe but very hard to carry home.

The German railroad had wide right-of-ways by their tracks, and they rented that land for the city people to have little patches of gardens to relax in or plant things. Those were their survival after the destruction of the city. After the attack, city water was quickly turned off to prevent any diseases from the contaminated water, which could turn out to be deadly for the few people left in the city.

* * * *

Friedl and Ilona noticed a change in Lizzi. She was very tired, listless, and looked like she had pain. The two sisters talked but thought, maybe the "not knowing" if her August was alive or would not come home again is weighing on her. Sometime during the latter part of 1946, Lizzi confided in Friedl that she was sick and worried but did not want to go to the hospital and leave the two girls all alone. Friedl explained to Lizzi that they had still Mrs. Nietsche, a true friend, and she would look after Friedl and Ilona.

The pain must have been getting worse. Lizzi made a trip to the family lawyer located now in a small village outside Darmstadt, and Friedl was sure she was not counting on August ever coming back. There were too many horror stories about the area that the Mongolians, the Russians, took over, like East Prussia, and a lot of the east border territory and the inhumane things these Russian military animals did. They had two weeks, given to the Russians by the Americans, to act out their horrendous deeds before General Eisenhower gave orders to move the American troops into Berlin. It was brilliant tactics on the part of the American army. Let the Russian army take the losses while "taming" Berlin. After, the American army could just march into the city.

So Lizzi was taking care of her beloved two girls, thinking that something might happen to her and the girls would need the lawyer's help and also would need money. When Lizzi got back from the lawyer's office, she told both her daughters that she established a trust for them and the family lawyer would take care of all their needs should she not make it.

Then Lizzi took care of herself and made her appointment with her physician at the same clinic where she gave birth to her babies. It was outside Darmstadt, but once the streetcar tracks were repaired, one could get there by streetcar. But that would be a while. One always could walk except for poor Lizzi, their precious mother.

Friedl and Ilona went by limousine with Lizzi to the clinic and to see her doctor. After Lizzi had some tests and an exam, she informed her girls how serious it all was. Lizzi had cancer, already spread to other organs. Surgery might help to lengthen her life, but there were no guarantees. Friedl and Ilona were in shock, could not speak, and just broke down crying.

Lizzi wanted to be brave but could not put on a good face either. The news was too terrible. Lizzi was only forty-six years old, still a beautiful and desirable woman. Besides, she would want to be there still, for her beloved girls and for her August when and if he would be coming home. Will the discouraging news ever stop? Will there ever again be a happy time and bring something good? Why did Lizzi and Katja survive this terrible war? At least the two sisters left have three beautiful girls to carry on. But Friedl and Ilona did not think the same. They did not want to carry on without Lizzi, their beautiful mother.

The day arrived, and their limousine was waiting outside. Lizzi, Mrs. Nietsche, and the girls were dressed and ready to take Lizzi to the clinic for surgery. Friedl and Ilona, the sisters, decided they would stay at the clinic. Nurses always have been so nice to them and offered beds to them before, so they would stay, just in case. In those years, the word *cancer* was taken as a death sentence.

It was a very cold and rainy day in November. Friedl and Ilona spent several days in the clinic chapel praying to God to save their beloved mother. One morning, as Friedl and Ilona were in the chapel praying, they were summoned by Lizzi's nurse to come and see the surgeon. He greeted them warmly and tried to console the two frightened girls as he was trying desperately to make the news a little gentler for them. But it was not the news they were praying for or had so hoped for. Their beloved Lizzi, their precious mother, had died during the surgery.

Both girls were devastated—all alone, their lives crumbled—and all around them was darkness. After arriving home by limousine, they sobbed and cried the rest of that day, saying and wishing if they could just have their beloved mother back, even in sickness, they wanted her to be with them. They would take good care of her and let her rest in bed—a desperate wish by two young lost girls, wanting to keep their mother under any circumstance.

Friedl still remembers that she and Ilona slept in their mother's bed that night, close together, comforting each other. The following day, they both went to see their family lawyer for him to arrange cremation and funeral of their beloved mother. The lawyer thought that he could arrange permission to put Lizzi's urn on top of Wolfgang's coffin, if at all possible. This would be a comforting thought for Friedl and Ilona to have their mother reunited with her only son for eternity.

The following years, Friedl and Ilona grew even closer, more so than ever before. They developed a close bond, a trusting relationship, and a psychologically and emotionally strong dependence on one another. There were now, after all, just the two of them.

A few months later, Friedl and Ilona received orders from their city government and the US occupation forces to vacate their home. Others as well in their neighborhood had to vacate. The notice stated that they would have forty-eight hours to take what they could carry or what they could transport.

After the bombings, the German government created an agency that would act in the behalf of the displaced people or the people who lost their homes in the bombing raids. These agencies now were taking care of the people from August and Lizzi's area, being displaced by American families coming into Germany for the duration of the officers' stay in Germany. Most have a two-year stay.

Friedl and Ilona were standing in their living room wondering what to take. "Something that is warm and fuzzy, perhaps? Something very valuable perhaps? But valuable to whom?" Ilona shouted, "My bear!" Their beds and bedding, their clothing, and their books—all were valuable to them.

Friedl chose her clothing, her bed and bedding, her books, and some pictures. Then they looked for something in memory of their mother, perhaps in the kitchen, one or all her baking books, all valuable to them, or maybe Lizzi's favorite tablecloths or some glasses, silver, or china they can use like the most precious sterling silver bowl that their father had given to Lizzi to thank her with this special gift after Friedl survived the complicated surgery that Lizzi insisted on and went by herself. Friedl treasured this special bowl and wanted to keep it in honor of her mother.

Dr. Hoffmann, across the street, who also had to vacate, was so very gracious and offered Friedl and Ilona his and his colleagues' help to move their beds and an armoire for their clothing and some other items the girls loved. Friedl and Ilona previously had been introduced to an elderly couple, Mr. and Mrs. Bogler, who had to give up one of their rooms for Friedl and Ilona. They had a flat with three rooms on the outskirts of the city. These buildings, only partially destroyed, had been already restored since the bombing in September 1944.

The Boglers, since they had no children, were allowed two rooms and had to surrender one room to the housing authority. At first, they resented Friedl and Ilona but after some time, after they got to know them and know a little more about them, began to not only tolerate Friedl and Ilona but also started to like the two young ladies.

In time, they became their family, their substitute parents. Friedl and Ilona liked living there and definitely enjoyed their company. They were not so alone any longer. Mrs. Bogler was generous and let them cook in her kitchen sometimes, provided they would keep it very clean and tidy. Otherwise, they had a little electric two-burner plate in their room to use. Friedl and Ilona's room, a beautiful light and large room, was to be their kitchen, living room, and bedroom. They had a certain allotted time for the use of the bath and had to pay for the hot water.

Mr. Bogler would invite the ladies some of the evenings into his study to relax in big chairs, and he would read aloud to Mrs. Bogler, Friedl, and Ilona. They enjoyed these evenings, a great reminder of their wonderful childhood that ended so abruptly and seemed a lifetime ago. "Such twisted roads life takes."

Those were delightful evenings in Mr. Bogler's study, a wonderful room with a veranda overlooking the courtyard and framed with flower boxes. The room was so bright and inviting. It had healing qualities. All the walls had built-in shelving clear to the ceiling, and it provided ample space for books. One must ponder how many books they would be invited to listen to before all this would change and they could have a reasonable and private life again. Was there a future, and what would it have in store for Friedl and Ilona? This thought that so often invaded their minds, especially at bedtime, was very frightening.

Friedl and Ilona would ride their bikes into the countryside, visiting farmers to beg for food. Sometimes, their journey would bring them to Katja's. She and Krimhilde were always delighted to see the two, Katja's beloved sister's girls. They always could count on Katja to provide dinner for them, and if they wanted to stay a little longer or overnight, they were welcome.

Some nights, the two would stay. The wonderful breakfast the next morning was beckoning. They had their own suite over the bakery, and that beautiful big soft bed was very inviting. On top of the mattress was a feather pillow as big as the mattress, a feather nest as it is called in Germany. One would practically disappear in it and to cover, another down comforter. Aunt Katja, before she would go to bed, would come and bring a tray with her hot chocolate and some Danish. She left it for the girls, said good night, and went to bed.

The next morning, Friedl and Ilona would wake up to the best smell in the world, bread and breakfast pastries. If the weather was nice, breakfast would be served in the back of the house, by the meadows with the apple and plum trees and a winding creek running through. The table was all set, and all four of them would sit down and enjoy the beginning of the day. After, Friedl and Ilona would be on their way back to Darmstadt. Never would Lizzi's girls have to leave without food.

One of those days, when Friedl and Ilona returned from a weekend in the country with their cargo of good food and unloaded their bikes to take it up to their room, they left their bikes leaning against the building. Ilona's bike was stolen. She exclaimed, "This is my livelihood, my way to get about." She needed her bike back, with no other way to travel into the country for food. The two girls searched for days in the neighborhood, a nearby park, no luck. They could not purchase a bike. There were no stores, and there was no other way to survive.

They went searching for a bike and found one in the rubble of a destroyed apartment building, part metal part rust, but it worked. Mr. Bogler had some brown paint, and Ilona painted the whole bike brown. She felt bad but talked herself into thinking that she only borrowed this bike and will take it back—later.

*   *   *   *

Nineteen forty seven came to an end, and Friedl and Ilona were invited to spend Christmas week and, if they wanted, longer, with Katja and Krimhilde. The girls were hoping for fair weather to be going by bike but found out that the train, leaving East Train Station, was now running. It was not far from Mr. and Mrs. Bogler, and they could walk there.

They took the train early Christmas Eve morning and got to Katja's for lunch. It was very nice spending Christmas again with their aunt and niece. There were plenty of food and sweets, but there also was that dark cloud that never had left. Friedl and Ilona did not know why they celebrated Jesus's birthday. By that time in their lives, Ilona especially did not believe in God any longer and was very bitter.

A few days into the New Year 1948, Friedl found out through the Red Cross that they heard a rumor, but they are not positive that their father, August, was a prisoner of war in a Russian prison camp in Siberia. She was told Red Cross would notify them when a special train with released prisoners would be coming through Darmstadt. Could there be hope?

It was September of 1948, and Ilona had a letter to mail to their friends in Switzerland, very good friends of August and Lizzi's, Walter and Sarah Christeler. In the makeshift post office in the center of the city in a burned-out building not yet restored, a big sign at the entry read, "German nationals, with the ability of reading, writing, and speaking English, please apply at the personnel office, IG Farben Building first floor, Frankfurt, daily from 0800 hours to 1300 hours."

Thinking back a few years, after Ilona's degree in International Law and Commerce, she would be working for an international firm. So why not now work for an international employer such as the United States Armed Forces. Her curiosity was aroused. How would she feel working for the victors and occupation force of her homeland? It aroused not only her curiosity but also her inquisitiveness.

This is three years after the war, and the American army is now the occupation force overseeing the rebuilding, not of the military power but of the infrastructure in their homeland. No longer are they the enemy.

She decided to go for it and asked her friend Hedy if she would be willing to risk it and join her. The two ladies went to Frankfurt to apply and complete their tests. In a few days, they were notified that they both got their jobs. Hedy was to start as a clerk in the provost marshal's office at headquarters in Frankfurt, and Ilona was to be a secretary to the radio communications officer, a colonel, at one of the garrisons in Darmstadt.

There was no transportation as yet in Darmstadt, no buses and no streetcars yet. The armed forces had two and a half ton (deuce-and-half) trucks, converted with benches inside and a ladder on the back hanging over the tailgate. They would pick up their German employees.

Friedl was worried with Ilona working right inside a garrison. Something could happen to her, and since she was the older one, she would be responsible for her. But after a discussion, Friedl gave in. The only worry Ilona had was that her beloved sister might be lonely now and miss her. But during the day, Friedl had Mrs. Bogler, and afternoons, Ilona would be back, and evenings, Mr. Bogler would return home.

After Ilona's first day on the job, her colonel invited her to watch a formal retreat, the lowering of the flag. It was for her an awesome sight, with these sharp, disciplined young soldiers marching up—no orders given, only silent command retrieving their flag. The flag was lowered as the band played the national anthem. The lowering of the flag was regulated, so the action was completed at the last note of the music. Ilona had goose bumps running down her spine as powerful as this scene was—and oh so bittersweet. That was the day her life meant something. It was the beginning of her new life!

After two months, everyone moved to the Northern Area Command headquarters in Frankfurt, but not the colonel. He got to go home. General Eisenhower occupied the headquarters building in Frankfurt. It was a beautiful building, an island in the midst of a wounded city—all marble, seven stories high with six wings. It was to be Ilona's home for the day and for years to come.

On one of those golden autumn Sundays, Friedl and Ilona with their bikes arrived in the country, and for the day, they were sightseeing. They were sitting outside a little café in a picturesque village having cold lemonade, and by a table next to them sat two very good-looking young men. One of the men was making eye contact with Friedl and smiled. In a while, he got the courage and came over to their table.

During the conversation, it was revealed that he worked at a haberdashery, a very fine one, Friedl remembered, before the bombing night of September 11, 1944. He and his family lost their home and were now living in the country. The other young man with him was his brother Heinz, and he was George. Well, after several trips on Sundays into the country to beg for food, they also would meet with George. He wanted to come to Darmstadt and take Friedl out.

That relationship went on for a few years, until George with his family and brother Heinz were able to come back to Darmstadt to live. The store, where George worked for in the past, also opened again, and George started his job as partner to the owner. Now that he had his job and profession back, he asked Friedl to marry him. Some paperwork had to be taken care of for Friedl and her former husband, Horst, who was declared as "died in action."

Friedl and George were married in 1950. They were a very handsome couple, very much in love. Ilona was very happy for her beloved sister and glad that Friedl found someone who loved her and would take care of her. However, there was still no word from the Red Cross about August, their father.

Times eventually did change, and the trains came back into service, and buses and streetcars started running again. Buildings were rising up, and stores would open, and one could get food now in the city. Ilona, walking home from the train station, was thinking that she no longer was in need of the borrowed bike, especially now being able to take the train to and from work. Trips to the country by bike for food were no longer needed. This was the chosen weekend when Ilona would take the bike back where she found it.

Saturday morning, Ilona started out with the bike by hand-pushing it while walking toward the city. She walked the same streets daydreaming of the day she had done that before in search of a bike. She walked by the former Marstall, the garrison where the grand duke once had his cavalry regiment and Ilona had her own horse stabled there. One can still see the horses' hooves imprinted on the sidewalk as they were trying to escape the burning stables.

Ilona's mind wandered, and she thought of the night of September 11, 1944. They were images of fire, a city in flames for many days, and as the Marstall was on fire, the horses not killed outright by the first bombs would be freed by the soldiers, their grooms, to run. They ran for their lives through the burning buildings out onto the streets or sidewalks. None of the horses nor the soldiers made it through. They had no way out. The whole city was on fire.

Ilona snapped out of it and kept pushing the bike. She finally came to the street and the bombed-out shells of apartment buildings. What once was an alley was now a terrace with flowerpots, and what was once a garage was transformed into a home now all fenced in with an iron fence and a gate. Ilona debated if she should just leave the bike outside the fence and leave.

At this moment, the gate opened, and a young blond man walked through, pushing a bike. That bike caught Ilona's eye. It was a Schwinn racing bike with chrome fenders and a fine red stripe on the frame and fenders. Behind the red leather seat was a little red leather pouch. This looked exactly like Ilona's bike; it *was* her bike! She could not speak! How could something like this happen? There is a one-in-a-million chance, she thought, to ever see her own bike again. The young man looked down at her, and with a smile, asked, "May I help you, are you looking for someone?"

Ilona regained her composure and said, "No, I am returning this bike I had borrowed." The young man told her that his twin brother had an old bike, all rusty, but no longer would need it, and that he died in the last few days of the war. His parents and younger sister died during the night of September 11, 1944, and when he returned from a prisoner-of-war camp, he did not have a bike either, but found one, leaning against a tree, this one.

By then, Ilona parked the borrowed bike and walked over to the young man holding her bike and looked at the back of the red leather pouch and saw her own initials, IE. Ilona did not have the heart to tell this young man that it was *her* bike. She felt so very sorry for him, gave him a nod, and, smiling, wished him a good day and walked away. It turned out that she did do a good deed today.

One early morning, Frederika (Friedl) and George drove up to Ilona's apartment building in George's father's little Volkswagen. George rang the bell, and Mrs. Bogler opened the door. "Don't pack too much," George called out as he was walking toward Ilona's door. "We have only my father's little car not a limousine." Ilona knew all about it and had asked for a week of vacation. It was an exciting trip that George had planned for Friedl, and Ilona was invited! This journey was in thought after so many, many years but so vivid still in Ilona's mind.

George and Ilona's precious sister, Friedl, so very happy and excited, sat in the front seat. Ilona and their little overnight bags were in the back seat, driving south on the auto route called the Road of Romance. Rothenburg, one of the most famous medieval towns in Germany, overlooked the Tauber Valley. It has retained its medieval character more than any other place: defense walls and towers, Gothic churches, monasteries, beautiful fountains, and Renaissance houses.

After exploring this picturesque place, taking photos, walking for hours, and getting hungry, they found an idyllic restaurant for lunch. Then they were on their way again, south. What a beautiful countryside, lovely scenery. They made their way past beautiful Ammersee Lake and Starnberger Lake where August kept his sailboat. They continued past Füssen and then to Hohenschwangau with a palace high above the Schwan Lake, the palace rebuilt by King Max II, with beautiful frescoes by Moritz von Schwind, then past Neuschwanstein's palace of King Ludwig II, built from 1869 to 1886. It had magnificent rooms with frescoes of motifs from Wagner operas. What a beautiful place to have concerts during the summer.

After a good night's rest from all the walking during the previous day, they drove through spectacular country along the Alpine auto route and headed for Bad (Bath) Reichenhall, one of the most beautiful Alpine health resorts and a world-renowned spa with forty-eight springs.

There they lingered for a few days, enjoying being spoiled by hotel staff, eating superlative food, and gazing at the shops in anticipation of a "little shopping excursion." While Friedl and George enjoyed being spoiled in the hotel, Ilona set out to do some shopping for them, little gifts in appreciation for taking her on this wonderful trip. Ilona found a beautiful, very slender and chic, white silk knit two-piece dress for Friedl. She would absolutely look stunning in it.

For George, Ilona found a tailored, brown silk shirt with patch pockets. Ilona, of course, could not resist as she passed by an attractive shop window offering Swiss hand-tailored garments, going in and browsing. It did not take her long to see, admire, and purchase a pale sea-green dress of Swiss cotton batiste. It fit perfectly, and it made such a small package. The storage area in the back seat of the car would hardly notice.

As it was almost time for dinner, Ilona went on her way back to the hotel with all her treasures. Friedl and George were waiting to go to dinner. It was a romantic setting, dinner served on the garden terrace. Candles were on each table and the waiters were dressed in tails, an outdoor orchestra playing Mozart.

The next morning, George and Friedl appeared, dressed in the beautiful garments Ilona had purchased for them. How grand they both looked. After a strong aromatic coffee and Danish, they took the cable railway up to the Predigtstuhl, a former Augustine monastery from the twelfth century with a beautiful and interesting Romanesque church, remodeled to late Gothic style with a large graveyard from the sixth and seventh century.

The three travelers returned to their hotel and got ready to continue their trip. Their next destination is Koenig See, king's lake south of Berchtesgaden, seventeen miles circumference, rugged limestone mountain faces rising up from the most beautiful deep blue waters of the lake. The famous pilgrimage church of Saint Bartholomae stood on the peninsula of Hirschau at one end of the lake. From a secluded vantage point, where painters would sit and paint this natural wonder, the three would relax and take in the breathtaking heights of the surrounding mountains and the deep beautiful water of this most spectacular of all lakes in the south of Germany, king's lake.

They had taken in all the sights, spent all the film for photos, and all good things have to come to an end. This holiday with Ilona's beloved sister, Friedl, and her George will remain in her memory, and when she dwells on it, she can recall everything in detail.

In 1952, the Red Cross notified Friedl that there was a prisoner-of-war train coming through Darmstadt. A few officers were to be on that train. Friedl had gone so many times to the train station she was getting frightened that it again would be, like all the other times, in vain. But Ilona told her that she would ask her colonel, for whom she worked, for a day off and after getting his OK would come with her. Both sisters, with high hopes, went to the train station and waited. Ilona, to break the silence and to make conversation because both were so scared, asked Friedl, "Do you think Father will recognize us?"

Friedl replied, "He will recognize you because you are an exact image of Lizzi." The train slowly came into the station and halted. The first soldiers debarked, and it was a shock to Friedl and Ilona. They were in rags; most of them did not even have shoes, and they all looked like ghosts. They looked just like skin over skeletons. It was a very gruesome sight to behold. Most of them, the girls assumed, would have been in prison, most likely before the war ended, years before, maybe ten or more years ago.

Then came some officers. They were dressed a little better. They still had part of their uniforms, no rags, but shoes. Friedl and Ilona looked at each other with a questioning look, their hearts pounding, when a man in very poor physical condition walked toward Ilona with a frown on his face but not speaking. So Ilona uttered one word, "Papa?" The prisoner nodded. Friedl and Ilona put their arms around this frail man and held him tight for a long while, sobbing. They helped him to the elevator and once outside the station called a taxi. During the taxi ride, it was mostly quiet, but August had some questions. Ilona was glad that Friedl answered. Ilona was quietly weeping inside and could not speak.

The question the two sisters were most afraid of came during the taxi ride. "Where is your mama? Where is my Lizzi? Why is she not here with you?" Ilona could not answer. Her throat was dry. She could not breathe and did not want to cry out.

Friedl answered, "My dearest Papa, your Lizzi, our precious mama was very sick, six years ago, with cancer. She had surgery and did not make it through. She left us. We are both so very sorry, Father. There was no way we could let you know. In fact, we did not know if you made it through the end of the war." There was silence in the car. Ilona and Friedl both looked at their father, and tears were streaming down his face.

He would not speak until they got to Friedl and George's apartment. All the news they had to convey to their poor father was bad. Friedl's husband, Horst, was killed going back to the Western Front, and she now is married to George, living in one room in a flat with two other families. Ilona still is living at the Boglers since their father's house was taken by the American army for American dependents. August's twin brother, Arthur, had committed suicide, and poor Lillie was back from a clinic living with her brother and sister. Christopher and Frieda along with their estate vanished during the siege of Berlin by the Russians. Katja's Philip had not returned from Stalingrad, and her little baby was now a beautiful red-haired, curly-headed young girl.

This news could not get any worse for their so very precious father. Their hearts were aching, yet they could not do anything for him, so they both got on their knees and hugged him. All three were sobbing.

The apartment their family along with Mrs. Kramer and Mrs. Nietsche occupied in the last two years of the war was again empty. The three families living in there had already found their own places, and Friedl and Ilona's father could move back in, after some repair work and painting, to make it nice and livable again. Friedl with Mrs. Nietsche would take care of their father, and George would look in on him every day.

Life in the beginning was hard on August especially his health. He had vascular problems, and sleeping on the dirt floor with one blanket all the years in Russian prison camp did make it worse. His legs had open areas and were very painful. But with doctor's care, good food, and a better life than the one in the prison camp, their father started to look again like himself. He was still a very handsome man.

When Ilona told him that she now was working for the American Armed Forces headquarters in Frankfurt, he had a sheepish smile on his face and said, "How did you get this job?"

Ilona told him the story, and her father raised his eyebrows saying, "That, my young lady, takes courage and in a language you did not care for! That makes me very proud." One day, he went to Frankfurt with Ilona to stop at Mercedes-Benz and inquire about a car. Maybe he would get another car now that he was feeling better.

He came to the IG Farben Building to meet his Ilona. She showed her father where she worked and introduced him to her colonel. They left her office and by cab went to the train station and together took the train home to Darmstadt. August ordered a new Mercedes-Benz in dove blue, with gray convertible top and gray leather inside. "It should arrive by Christmas," her father told Ilona on the train ride home. He sounded excited, and Ilona was happy for her father. She wanted to see him happier than he has been.

"This is something very nice to look forward to," she said with a smile toward her father.

The new car for August was not the only news. Friedl and George were awaiting another baby. The little girl Christina they welcomed a little over a year ago before had died due to an epidemic that spring. Many infants died of that virus.

Christmas was coming, and Ilona had already asked at work to have a day off when her sister would have her baby. It was all set. Their father was taking the bus to Frankfurt to pick up his new "baby." This could turn out to be the best Christmas they all had in many years.

Ilona received a phone call at her desk from a hospital in Frankfurt, which informed her of an accident between a bus and a passenger car (her father's new car). The driver was seriously injured. She was asked if she could please come to the hospital for additional information. Ilona went to see her father. It looked like he might not make it. She did not know how to break this to Friedl, not to upset her since she was close to the time to having her baby.

Ilona had requested to have her father transported to Darmstadt if it would not endanger him. In a few more days, they were able, by ambulance, to transport August to the hospital in Darmstadt. Friedl was able to see and visit her father. A few more days passed. August's condition was still serious but not critical any longer, and it was time for his daughter Friedl to join him in the same hospital to await her little one.

It was now December 23, and Ilona had the phone call she was expecting from George. She had permission to leave work early and catch the train to Darmstadt, and she went directly to the hospital to visit her father and then to visit Friedl and the new arrival, Joachim, a little boy child in time for Christmas. Ilona was thinking, *It is about time for some good news in her family. It's Christmas early!*

George came after work, and they could celebrate Christmas together the next day. Maybe their father could join Friedl in her room for a while. If the sisters, the nurses, would be able to do this, and George, Friedl with baby, their father, and Ilona all could have Christmas Eve together. Ilona would bring the gifts, some candles, and goodies, and they could celebrate Christ and Joachim's birthdays all together as a family. Mrs. Nietsche was also invited since she was hired now to take good care of August once he would be released from the hospital. She came later on Christmas Eve and brought two little Christmas trees with little candles for Friedl and the baby and for August.

* * * *

The New Year 1953 brought many surprises and happy moments. August was feeling good again and looked very good. One afternoon, he came back from his walk and told his girls he got himself a first-class ticket to Bern, Switzerland, to visit his dear friends, the Christelers. It had been such a long time since he had seen them before and one time during the war. They lived in Lenk by Bern, and before retiring, they had the factory that made the famous Käthe Kruse dolls. Ilona had one, but hers stayed with the house.

In later years, Friedl bought Ilona another one. Ilona was slated to marry their son someday, but that did not work out. Ilona did not show any interest, and Walter Jr., their son, after trying, gave up. On the way to Switzerland, their father would stop at Lake Starnberg, where his beautiful sailing vessel *ANMUT* was moored. All these past ten years, their father had not been there to see his friends and his boat. It will be a wonderful trip for their father and also a little rest and relaxation for him. Friedl, George, and Ilona did not ask August how long he would be gone. It is after all a vacation for him with no strings.

Ilona after the Christmas holiday and New Year went back to work in Frankfurt, looking forward to her job and the wonderful people around her. There was something new. A new group of radio communications personnel and their commanding officer were moved into the adjacent rooms to theirs, new equipment, among a facsimile machine where they would receive materials, even pictures in an instant.

From December 23 to now was a lot of change. Ilona's phone rang every morning, a message to the new commanding officer Captain Richards, from his Sgt. Halvor LeGrand Cole to report on the status of the installation of radio equipment at Hohes Lohr, a mountaintop with a new radio tower and radio equipment to be installed by the Firm Lorenz located near Bad Wildungen.

After some time, Ilona was talking to her friend Hedy, telling her of that beautiful voice she heard calling every morning. She wondered what the man behind it would look like? Well, he had called again but from here in Frankfurt to report to the captain. Hedy and Ilona had coffee in the snack bar together, and she told Hedy about it, all excited. Hedy said, "Ah, with a wave of her hand, he is short, fat, and bald!"

"No, no," said Ilona. "The man belonging to that voice is not short or fat, bald is all right." Well, well, they both will find out very soon.

Ilona's office handling all Top Secret and Classified material had an MP (military police) outside her door with a rifle over his shoulder. Her old and beautiful desk was right inside that door.

It was on a Monday morning: The MP stepped aside, the door opened, and a young soldier, a sergeant, walked through the door, smiled, and as he saw his commanding officer stood at attention with a sharp salute, announced, "Sergeant Halvor LeGrand Cole reporting, Sir!" Ilona recognized this voice—it sounded very familiar—"It is he!"

During the conversation between the sergeant and his commanding officer, Captain Richards and Ilona's colonel, Sergeant Cole, sat on Ilona's desk. With her finger waving and a smile, he seemed to catch the message. No one sits on her desk. It was a beautiful highly polished old desk, most likely left from better times before the war, belonging no doubt to an executive at IG Farben. It had most likely a deeper meaning than it was Ilona's desk, if only for eight hours of the day, but it was all hers! Ilona did not have to share it with someone nor did she have to ask if she could use it. It was at that time and place her only possession.

Sergeant Cole got up, turned around to face Ilona, got a hold of his tie, and leaned over, looking her in the eye with a smile on his face, his beautiful hazel eyes shining, and wiped the spot where he sat. Well, Halvor LeGrand Cole and Ilona met this moment, this day. The flirting and admiration between them began.

Sergeant Cole was transferred to Frankfurt from Hohes Lohr to supervise and run this new radio communications group and also the radio sites, Frankfurt, Wiesbaden, Darmstadt, and Bad Kreuznach. He came to the office every morning to report to Captain Richards and then left to go to his sites.

Some afternoon, after returning from his travels, he came by Ilona's desk and asked, "Ilona, would you like to have a cup of coffee upstairs in the snack bar?" She had a break coming and agreed. When they were sitting, sipping their coffee, Sergeant Cole asked Ilona if she would mind if he asked her to take him to see the sights in Frankfurt since he just recently arrived in the city. "But no GI places," Sergeant Cole added.

Ilona of course was willing to spend some evenings with this charming and handsome young man, showing him the sights of Frankfurt. Ilona did not know of any GI places, bars, and such, where American soldiers would frequently go. Ilona thought for a moment and said, "We can go for a nice walk along the river and come back toward the city where I know of a fine restaurant, newly rebuilt, and there are no American GIs."

Sgt. Halvor LeGrand Cole then asked Ilona to please call him Hal. This was Ilona's first time she broke her own promise to herself not to socialize with people she worked with and especially not with any soldier. Ilona left herself some leeway and broke her own promise, smiling. That evening, they strolled along the Main River. One could see all the twinkling lights of the city of Frankfurt. And then they went to a very fine restaurant for only German patrons, no soldiers allowed. It was called the Kaiser Keller (emperor cellar).

Even though Hal had his uniform on (since he was not yet allowed to be in civilian clothes) since Germany was still occupied, the waiter seated them, and they had excellent service. When they left, they told Hal, "Good night, Sir, please come again."

Ilona and Hal had no difficulty in any of the German places they picked. Hal and Ilona picked another evening for a date, and Hal asked Ilona, "Would you mind if I bring Henry along the next time?"

Ilona thought it strange and with a smile said, "Yes, it is fine with me." This was the following Saturday, and Hal met Ilona outside the Kaiser Keller.

After they greeted each other, Hal pulled a pipe out of his pocket and said, "Meet Henry." Hal wanted to know if a pipe would be allowed.

"Of course," Ilona said, smiling. That evening, when they parted, Hal asked Ilona if she would like to go dancing some evening. He was full of surprises, that Sgt. Halvor LeGrand Cole—not fat, not short, not bald, and he could dance! Ilona had to have a talk with Hedy and straighten her out. "Yes, I love to dance. This would be so nice, and I will look for a very nice nightclub where we can go," Ilona answered. Ilona also knew now how her mother, Lizzi, felt between the formal dances after meeting her August. The weeks were too long, the weekends or the evenings of the ball too short. Ilona felt the same way.

They saw each other at the office most days when Hal would come by her desk to speak with Captain Richards; but on a Saturday night or Sunday afternoon, being with him, talking with him, or just sitting there looking at him was very different and oh so special.

Saturday came, and Ilona, all dressed up, was ready to take the train to Frankfurt and meet Hal. He was waiting at the train station as the train rolled in. His beautiful smile told Ilona he was looking forward to this evening with her too. Speaking of that extra heartbeat, Ilona had it as she was walking toward him. They walked from the train station up Kaiser Strasse and looked into shops; and as they continued, Hal took Ilona's hand in his, and they walked to the nightclub, the Huetten Bar.

As they entered, they were again greeted by a gentleman who was very friendly and courteous. Walking down the stairs and into the club, all eyes there turned to them. A German club, an American in uniform, and a German lady? Again, they would make a good impression and would be asked to come back. They had a wonderful time dancing and having champagne. The orchestra was playing all kinds of music, tango, waltzes, slow waltz, rumba, and samba. Hal and Ilona's favorite music and dance was "Blue Spanish Eyes" and the "Blue Tango."

In the future, when Hal and Ilona came in, the orchestra would stop what they were playing and start with the "Blue Tango." It turned out to be their two favorite places: the Kaiser Keller and the Huetten Bar. Hal was telling Ilona that he had a birthday coming and wanted to spend it with her. For not wanting to get involved with an American soldier, Ilona already had that extra heartbeat and a much deeper feeling for Hal. She wanted to give him something beautiful, something he could take home and remember her by. Since Hal was smoking a pipe, it was easy. She went to a jewelry store and purchased a sterling-silver pipe lighter and had Hal's initials engraved on it.

The birthday came, and they met in Frankfurt at the train station. They took the streetcar to the Palm Garten, a beautiful park near the Opera with palm trees and pathways, a beautiful lake with swans, and a wonderful café. They walked around for a while, took pictures of each other, and then went to the café to have coffee and apple tarts. They walked again along the Main River, like they did on their first date, and sat on a bench for a while to talk. Hal was telling Ilona about his family, his siblings, his sister Bev and brother Doug, both quite a bit younger than him. He was telling sweet stories about his puppy at home named Rusty.

When it was time for dinner, they walked toward the city and came to the Kaiser Keller. After they were seated, Hal ordered some wine, and while they were toasting Hal's birthday, Ilona gave Hal his birthday present. Hal seemed very happy about it since it was a gift he really would use. They talked of travelling, and Ilona told Hal the places she went to on summer vacations. Hal asked, "Have you ever considered going to the United States?"

Ilona, surprised about this question, said, "Oh no, it is really too far."

After a moment, Hal looked at her and, smiling, said, "As my wife?"

Ilona was surprised and taken aback by that question and did not know how to answer or what to say. Hal noted Ilona's indecision, but he could also see she was surprised and stunned.

After dinner, outside, Ilona turned to Hal and said, "Could you ask me the question again?"

Hal repeated it, and Ilona gave him a kiss on the cheek and said yes. The real kiss—the first kiss between them—came later, as they said goodbye at the train station. Warm waves came over Ilona, and she knew at that moment that if she did not feel love for Hal before, she surely loved him now.

It was hard to say goodbye again, and as Hal walked away, she had some tears in her eyes, wondering where this would lead her.

Ilona thought it was time to own up to this relationship since it was getting more and more serious. It was time for Hal to meet her family. Ilona had no opposition from George. He was all for it to meet this man Ilona was serious about! It was her sister who needed convincing that Hal was a wonderful young man and really loved Ilona. George put in a few good words to Friedl, and Ilona made some points too, and Friedl agreed to invite Papa, and they would have afternoon coffee and a piece of torte and meet this young man.

Ilona took an early train to Frankfurt to meet and accompany Hal to her sister's house. They took the train down to Darmstadt on that Sunday afternoon. On the train, Hal would not sit down, standing all the way. Ilona said a few times, "Honey, please sit down. The people won't mind. There is plenty room for you."

Later, Hal admitted that he did not want to rumple his trousers since he was meeting her father. They both got along well, and August liked Hal right away and conversed with Hal in English. The afternoon looked like it was all coming together, and Ilona was relieved that all went well. Friedl too liked Hal very much. Serious conversation about all this would come for Ilona with her father later when August found out there would be a wedding and his Ilona would, after that, move to America.

Two months later, it was Ilona's birthday, and they sat outside in the beautiful garden at the Kaiser Keller with an orchestra playing while Hal gave Ilona a little box. He ordered a bottle of wine, and while they were waiting for their dinner, Ilona opened the box. It was the most beautiful diamond ring. In fact, it was the ring that Ilona admired a few weeks ago in the jeweler's window. "How did you know the size?" Ilona asked. "I had no idea that you wanted to buy that ring."

During dinner, Hal wanted to talk about something important. Papers! "Papers we have to submit to the State Department and the American Armed Forces to get permission for us to get married," said Hal with anticipation in his voice. "It is important that we start now. It takes the army a while, and since my time in the army is up in December, it is important to get serious now."

To that, Ilona remarked, "Since I already have clearance for working with Top Secret and Classified material, it should not take too long."

Hal had already asked the State Department for the papers and brought them to the office so they could start to fill them out. There were more than just papers. There were doctor's appointments for Ilona, for blood tests, and then to the dentist's for checking teeth. They also needed a marriage certificate of Ilona's parents and Ilona's birth certificate. All had to be submitted and translated into English, six copies of each. Ilona was not allowed to do the translating. The consulate had to do this and charged Ilona per line.

The next five months were very busy with papers, certificates, appointments, and translations. But it was needed if Hal and Ilona wanted to get married. But with all this to take care of, Hal and Ilona saw each other often. There were many nice dinners at the Kaiser Keller, wonderful evenings dancing close together at the Huetten Bar, and some very exciting train trips along the Rhine River, the wine country, and boat tours along the Rhine River through spectacular scenery and stops to taste wine.

Ilona's friend Sigi—who was transferred to Bad Godesberg with HICOG, the American High Command—invited Hal and Ilona to come and visit her. They had a wonderful afternoon with Ilona's friend and an evening of dancing. Sigi also agreed to be Ilona's bridesmaid.

Mr. Blieske, one of the German engineers at Ilona's department, had a house right outside Frankfurt. He was going to give a party for Hal and Ilona and invited all the employees, officers, and enlisted personnel to participate. Captain Richards brought his wife. She was living in Frankfurt for the duration of Captain Richards's two-year duty.

Two American civilians working in the office came, along with Ilona's colonel. It was a large party room that Mr. Blieske had built in his basement. The ceiling was painted white, and there were black footprints going across the ceiling. If one knew Mr. Blieske, one would understand his humor. That evening was very memorable, and everyone enjoyed the mixing of two worlds and were getting along splendidly.

Time passed and it was time to think of a bridal gown and all the necessities a wedding required. Ilona designed her wedding gown and had it sewn by the dressmaker who did all her clothes. The paperwork was on the way. They had done their part, and now, it was just waiting.

Sigi came down from Bad Godesberg on a weekend so Ilona could take her shopping. It was German custom for the bride to buy all the things a bridesmaid needed for the wedding. That meant the dress, undergarments, stockings, and shoes. The two ladies had fun shopping together and after, going to a café and having coffee and a piece of torte. Ilona also got the items she would need for that special day.

Hal met the two ladies in Frankfurt on the Hauptwache. It is the center of Frankfurt, and they walked across to Café Kranzler, a wonderful place. Waiters, white table linens, a musician walking around playing the violin, and all the tortes, cakes, and tarts and wonderful coffee—everything one's heart could desire. Hal and Ilona accompanied Sigi to the train station. There they all parted. Ilona's train went to Darmstadt, Sigi's train went to Bad Godesberg, and Hal took a cab to bring him to his barracks in Frankfurt.

Monday morning, as Ilona arrived at her office, there was an envelope addressed to her on her desk. It was from Hal and had a note in it explaining why he could not come by the IG Farben Building and speak to her to tell her in person. He was ordered to come to the office very early and sign out a car to go to Karlsruhe that day.

Karlsruhe was the city where Hal's company headquarters was located, and he would report there to his superior officer, who was higher than Captain Richards. Hal asked Ilona in the note if she could stay in Frankfurt after work and maybe take a later train.

Ilona, after her day of work, waited upstairs in the lobby of the building for Hal to arrive. Since it was a beautiful evening, Ilona sat outside the IG Farben building on a bench. Two hours later, Hal arrived and invited Ilona to come to dinner with him at the Kaiser Keller. As they were still by the bench, a gentleman walked by, commenting, "What a beautiful couple you make. May I take your picture?" Hal always had his camera with him and handed it to this nice gentleman.

Hal and Ilona photographed by a kind stranger

While they were waiting to order and were sipping on a glass of champagne, Hal told Ilona, "I went to Karlsruhe today to have a meeting with my superior officer, Colonel Genebach, to give him our paperwork and ask for permission to marry you, a German national. And of course, he said yes! You have a meeting scheduled with the provost marshal's office, a Colonel Adenetto, tomorrow at 1700 hours upstairs in the IG Farben Building." Hal held both of Ilona's hands in his, smiled at her, and asked, "You are not scared, are you?"

Ilona had seen this colonel before. He did not look scary, so Ilona answered, "But, hopefully, he does not slur or speak too fast. That usually scares me. I am worried I can't catch all he is saying."

The evening was relaxing, and Hal seemed happy with his accomplishment that day. Ilona had some good news too. She had an offer from a coworker to rent a room in her flat and could live in Frankfurt, just long enough to take care of everything until the wedding.

Ilona got very little sleep, going out with Hal after work and taking the later train home to Darmstadt and coming back early in the mornings by train to her office. She also would get a little more rest since she shared a room at her sister's with the baby, and sleeping some nights came in little doses since the baby often awoke and cried. Ilona hoped the appointment with Colonel Adenetto would turn out well.

When he found out that Ilona had been working here at headquarters as secretary to the communications officer, his face took on a different demeanor, although he did want to test this German lady. He asked, "Why do you wish to go to the United States?"

Ilona gave him the right answer, judging by his face. "It is not a wish of mine to go to the United States. It is the home of the man I fell in love with. It so happened that this man is from the United States. I would go with him anywhere to live."

Well, Ilona got his seal of approval that afternoon. When Ilona would see Colonel Adenetto in the hallways or the snack bar, he would always stop and greet her in a friendly way.

Hal came into the office and stopped by Ilona's desk one morning, beaming like a child on Christmas. "The letter came with the permission for us to get married, and the date is November 14," Sgt. Halvor LeGrand Cole said to his beloved Ilona. "Can you take a break and come up to the snack bar and I buy you a coffee and a Danish? We have to set the date with the German authorities so our marriage will be legal in the eyes of the German government," he announced to Ilona.

Hal seemed so excited. Ilona had not seen this before. Ilona looked at her Hal, smiled at him, and said, "We can go to the courthouse the day before and have Sigi and your friend join us there and have our ceremony, and after, take them to dinner."

The date was set. On Friday, the thirteenth of November, Hal and Ilona would be married for the German law; and on Saturday, the fourteenth of November, they would be married in the American chapel in Frankfurt for American law.

On one of the nice sunny Sundays in autumn, Hal and Ilona made a date with Friedl to take Joachim, her baby son, out for a walk with the baby carriage. They wanted to first have some fun with the older generation of Germans and, second, to take the baby off Friedl's hands for a day, since she was pregnant with another child and could use the rest.

Hal, still in his uniform, met Ilona at Friedl's, and together they walked with the baby carriage through the Herren Garten, a beautiful park with a café located in it, which was frequented by "elderly German ladies." Hal and Ilona made a bet as to how many looks of disdain Hal and Ilona would receive and looks of contempt for a baby.

It turned out to be a fun afternoon, and quite a few "old ladies" surprised them by coming closer and admiring the baby boy, with some even saying, "Oh, what a beautiful baby. He just looks like his mommy." When they were back at Friedl's home, they told her what happened, and George and everyone got a good laugh over this.

Everything was now set—the date, the announcements and the invitations, Ilona's dress, Hal's tuxedo from Friedl's husband, George, and reservations for out-of-town guests.

The day arrived, the thirteenth of November, a Friday. The ceremony was short but nice, and dinner was lively with Sigi and Hal's buddy. After dinner, Hal and his best man went by cab back to the barracks, and Sigi and Ilona went to her flat in the city. The next day would be the day Hal and Ilona considered their wedding day.

Everyone was there, friends and some family of Ilona's and their coworkers and superiors. The only one missing was August. He did not want to attend or give his Ilona away. Ilona was depressed about that and was very anxious about the ceremony. She worried that she might not be able to follow the chaplain's words and their guests in the front seats might laugh about it. The ceremony went well, but Ilona was stressed and did not hear the chaplain's words when he said, "You may now kiss the bride."

So when Hal turned toward Ilona, pulled her close, and got ready to kiss her, Ilona stiffened up and almost took a step backward, saying, "What are you doing, Sgt. Halvor LeGrand Cole?" This American custom was unknown to Ilona, but it all worked out.

*   *   *   *

Hal and Ilona's Wedding Kiss

Halvor LeGrand Cole in his civilian clothes

The next day, before Mr. and Mrs. Cole left for their honeymoon, they stopped at the American consulate to start the papers for Ilona's visa, her entry papers to the United States. It would take three months. For their honeymoon, they took a train to Switzerland. Their first stop was Basel. They left their luggage in lockers at the train station and went sightseeing in the city, stopped and had lunch, and then went on to Bern. They checked into their hotel and stayed for two days. They went to the museum and the beautiful old cathedral. They watched old gentlemen play garden chess—large chess figures on a huge chessboard on the grass in the park. They went to dinner the first night and had spaghetti with a delicious sauce and a bottle of Chianti wine, very casual.

After the second day in Bern, they went by train to Lucerne, a beautiful very old city, right in the midst of the Alpine Mountains by a large dark blue lake, Vierwaldstaettersee (Lake Lucerne). After checking into their hotel, they went for a walk and spotted the old wooden chapel bridge, 670 feet long, crossing the Reuss River. It was the oldest wooden bridge in Europe, built in 1333. All through the bridge, up against the rafters, were paintings depicting the history of Lucerne and of Switzerland.

The next morning, Hal and Ilona purchased tickets for a boat ride and a mountain train, a locomotive with about two or three passenger cars, open, crawling up the mountainside on tracks. They passed alpine meadows, cows grazing, and a lot of wildflowers, until they got higher up the mountain and snow appeared. They went up all the way to the summit. The view was breathtaking; below were the white clouds, and they were surrounded by high mountaintops, snow glistening silver in the sun.

They took pictures, especially of Hal in civilian clothes, looking handsome but quite different from his uniform. They entered a beautiful restaurant high on this mountaintop. Hal ordered the special cheese plate and a bottle of wine. The waiter brought to the table the largest platter they had ever seen of a wonderful variety of cheeses they enjoyed with their wine and conversation.

As the evening approached, Hal and Ilona took the train back down the mountain and took the boat back to Lucerne and their hotel. The next day, they went by train to Zurich. After they returned from their sightseeing and shopping, they noticed a cozy corner in the hotel bar. They sat down and noticed that there was a menu for late lunch or early dinner on the table in front of them. Hal ordered for them some toast squares and foie gras with a consommé and a glass of champagne. They ended their meal with an espresso.

Next day, their destination was Garmish, a ski resort in the Alps. Going out that evening, exploring this picturesque little town, Hal and Ilona found a nightclub that looked very intriguing. After they had dinner with a very nice bottle of aged red Burgundy, the dance floor moved back to show an ice rink instead, and Hal and Ilona watched, to their amazement, the most beautiful ice show. It was a wonderful finish to their honeymoon.

The next day, the train brought them back to Frankfurt and reality. When Hal entered his barracks, one of his buddies saw him and told him that his orders came through while he was away. The army and his commanding officer, Captain Richards, were looking for him. "Of course, if no one were to see you," said the corporal, "you could not be reached and spend one more day with your bride, sir." Hal and Ilona had one more day!

They went to their favorite café to enjoy a cup of good coffee and a piece of torte, talking about all kinds of unimportant subjects to avoid the very obvious, parting! The door to the café opened, and a captain entered. It was Captain Richards! He walked past Hal and Ilona, did not acknowledge them, hung up his cap, and sat down in a corner. This grateful couple, of course, had the rest of that day off, so they left.

It was December 6 in Germany, a celebration for Saint Nicholas, and little gifts are given. Friedl put on Christmas early for Hal since Hal was leaving and, therefore, could not celebrate Christmas with them. They exchanged gifts, and after a little celebration, Ilona accompanied Hal to the train station. He would start his journey to

Karlsruhe, where Hal had to report to his company, and then a train would bring Ilona's dear husband through Frankfurt.

The train would stop there for about one hour, Hal told Ilona, and she would go to the train station to see her beloved Hal one more time before the train would make the journey to Bremerhaven, where a ship would be waiting to take him to the United States and home. "Why is there always sadness connected to happiness?" Ilona asked her dear sister Friedl when she moved back to Darmstadt again.

Ilona was trying to break the ice and think of something special to send to Hal's mother, her future mother-in-law. She would be greeting a stranger. She was not asked if her son could marry this woman, nor did she have any input in decision-making. Ilona went to the florist and ordered one dozen red roses to be sent to Mrs. Halvor W. Cole in Seattle, to be delivered on December 23. *Maybe this will smooth the way*, she thought.

Ilona kept on working, taking the train. She wrote letters to her Hal and received letters from him. February arrived, and Ilona received her visa. Shortly after, Hal sent Ilona a TWA ticket to fly to Seattle. Ilona surely had mixed feelings. She never really thought that through. She would be happy to be reunited with her husband but also very sad to be leaving her family, especially her Friedl.

After work, she walked to the train station and stopped in at the TWA airline office to pick up her ticket. Ilona was crying all the way to the train station and in the train all the way to Darmstadt. Upon arriving at her sister's door, she saw that Friedl was doing the same thing, most likely all that day.

Ilona had some serious talks with August, her beloved father, but he could not see why she would have to leave. Could Hal not stay in Germany? He had a very desirable and needed profession in telecommunication, which was especially needed now in Germany. August would pay to have Hal take courses and learn German, and August would take care of all the costs. He would purchase a nice flat for them in Frankfurt. Why would Ilona want to leave her dear sister? August just could not understand his precious daughter. Ilona thought it best not to get into this conversation again.

Ilona continued working, thinking this way, the time would go by faster; and this way, she would not be confronted by her father. Ilona put her resignation in for the twenty-fifth of February, since on the twenty-sixth, she would be going to the Frankfurt Rhine-Main Airport to board her plane that would bring her, after thirty-six long hours, to Seattle and her beloved husband.

*   *   *   *

"Portland, Oregon. Next stop, Seattle, Washington!" the captain announced as the plane was landing in Portland. It was an awesome sight from above. All the twinkly lights over this city, it was beautiful. Will Seattle look this pretty? Will the whole family be at the airport? Ilona was hoping not, the way she felt after this long flight. *Just my Hal*, she told herself. A second later, she thought, *if they are not there, they most likely don't like me and don't want to meet me.* All this was stirring around in Ilona's brain until the landing. Yes, Seattle looked just as beautiful at night as Portland, and bigger. Ilona had to debark on the tarmac and walk to the terminal.

Above by a large window, she saw her sweetheart and, one, two, three, four people next to him. "They are *all* there," she was whispering to herself. The greeting went well. Hal had a nice family. This should not be too difficult to be accepted by them especially if Ilona will prove that she loves Hal very much and is a good wife. This should be rather easy since she loves Hal so much that she left her home and family for this special man. Hal had borrowed his father's car, and they all went in two cars to their family home.

After some talk and many questions, Hal and Ilona left for their apartment on Capitol Hill on Bellevue Avenue North. Hal and Ilona would not have a car for a while, but Hal could borrow his father's if he would need one. He was taking the bus downtown to the telephone building. They walked up the stairs and entered the flat. It looked very inviting. Hal, his mother, and his sister Bev had done a beautiful job fixing it up with some rented furniture, and drapes were put up on all windows. The kitchen was already all outfitted, so Ilona could start breakfast for Hal in the morning. It had a nice big bath and had a walk-in closet.

The previous renter had his bed permanently put into the closet, and this was Hal and Ilona's bedroom now. It was nice and light with a good-sized window in it. It was a wonderful apartment, and after many years of sharing one room with her sister, for Ilona, this was now paradise! She would take her key after Hal left for work and walk down into the lobby to turn around and go back up, walk in, push the door shut, and shout, "This is all mine, all mine!"

"This morning, it is time to call George," Ilona told Hal as he was leaving for work. She had promised and asked George if it would be all right to call him at work. They did not have as yet a phone in their new home. Ilona called George, tears stuck in her throat, but at least, she could give her beloved sister this message: "I arrived safely in Seattle. Hal and his family picked me up, and now, we are in a very pretty apartment in Seattle. Tell Friedl I will call on Sunday at Aunt Lillie's at three o'clock afternoon, your time. Lillie knows about it already and is expecting you and Friedl. Hopefully, I will be able to get through. Give my mouse a big hug and a kiss from me and Hal. Take care of my beloved sister, and tell her that Hal and I are both fine, and I miss her."

Before they hung up, George was telling Ilona that the night she was flying to Seattle, Friedl gave birth to a little boy named Rainald. "Friedl and baby are doing fine," added George before he hung up.

* * * *

February in Seattle is mostly wet. It was raining every day. Ilona got bored and wanted to find a job. First, she was afraid to walk too far away from the apartment, but soon, she realized that she could remember markers, a certain building—left turn, or an intersection with certain buildings—going straight. This would not be different than in any country in unfamiliar cities.

Ilona went to the employment office in downtown Seattle and applied. They sent her to the Bon Marche for an office job. After she had passed the test, she was called in to have an interview with a gentleman. He was very nice at first until he found out where Ilona came from and said to her, "I have to hire *my own* people first, sorry." Ilona left, crying and very discouraged about this interview, and went home. Finding the street and her apartment was a minor glitch on this day.

After some time, after Ilona gathered her courage again, she went for another interview. It was in Downtown Seattle in one of the better neighborhoods by the train station on First Avenue. It was called Bank Check Supply. They printed the checks for the banks and hired Ilona to work with invoices. Ilona liked her job and her bosses, two brothers. She went by bus, and after they had a car, Hal would drop her off.

One morning, as she approached her office building, she almost stumbled over a bundle of clothing. As she stepped back, she realized that this bundle was not clothing but a human being. Upset that he would be lying there and no one paid attention to him or get some help, she ran up the stairs to the office and announced it to her coworkers. They, of course, being used to this happening, laughed and told Ilona that the man downstairs is sleeping off his wine, that he is drunk.

A year later, the company moved to Broadway in the Capitol Hill area to a new location close to Hal and Ilona's apartment building, and Ilona was able to walk to work. "This is much nicer, new offices and walking to work in an area where it was safe to walk," Ilona told Hal. Ilona could enjoy walking home after work and stopping for groceries. Two big supermarkets were on her way home.

During the time they lived in Seattle, they had the opportunity to move into another apartment, on the same floor, but a one-bedroom apartment. Ilona and Hal liked it there, and this would give them a little more room. Letters and pictures of Friedl and the two boys were coming regularly, and Ilona was writing letters at least once a week and also lots of pictures. This was how these two sisters who loved each other very much bridged the far distance.

Hal came home one day with the good news of a promotion. Ilona was very proud of him, considering his age. But then he was always very mature and responsible. Hal and Ilona decided to start buying their own furniture, not much but some they could call their own. Hal had heard that there was a GI loan available should he want to buy a home. He was all excited, and he and Ilona searched for a nice lot to have a little house built.

For Ilona, that sounded exciting to see—how, here in America, they would construct their houses. They would go up so fast and were entirely made of wood or man-made wood products, and they all looked very similar. One had a house built by the number of bedrooms and bathrooms, which were not necessarily bathrooms. They mostly were small rooms, maybe with a tub in it or a shower and a toilet, right in the same room, and a sink. If only a toilet is in the room, they still call it a bathroom.

It is very different, but the houses look very pretty and are mostly one-story high, which makes them look so nice. Ilona liked that style. Their gardens are all around their houses, but they are sometimes nice and green and sometimes brownish. Ilona found out why. They fertilize that grass they call lawn, and as soon as it grows, someone with a machine they call a lawn mower cuts it off. Then they start over and they fertilize to make it grow. When it does, they cut it off again as short as a crew cut. If one drives through neighborhoods, one will see them work on their garden in the summer every evening and weekends. No wonder, all that extra effort, why?

*   *   *   *

In November 1955, Hal and Ilona moved into their new very pretty little house. Hal started his new job with AT&T in North Bend, a little village on the way to the Cascade Mountains. The phone company had built a new building there with all new more modern and updated equipment, and Hal was the manager of a handpicked group of six men.

Now Hal had to drive every day since there were no buses going to North Bend. Ilona had not learned to drive yet and, therefore, had to end her job at Bank Check Supply. Eventually, Ilona got her driver's license and found a job with a bank (Seattle First National Bank) not too far from their house on Mercer Island, a very charming little village right by the beautiful Lake Washington.

Hal and Ilona were very busy with their jobs and also decorating their house inside with beautiful furniture, a few art pieces, and lovely china from Ilona's home in Germany. The house looked beautiful with Hal and Ilona's different touches and tastes. Hal and Ilona were happy, a very devoted and loving couple. Life was now so very precious and wonderful for them.

Ilona could not believe as she came into the house from the mailbox holding a letter and could not take her eyes off the return address. She called out to Hal, "You won't believe this, honey. I have here a letter from my father!" Hal came from his library to the kitchen and gave Ilona a big hug, holding her tight and saying, "It has to be only good news. Why else would your father write to you?"

They opened the letter, and as Ilona started to read, she started crying and tried to tell Hal that her beloved father has forgiven her for leaving. She has truly stayed in touch with her precious sister, Friedl, and after much contemplating and thinking it over, he, her father, has forgiven her and is asking for Ilona's forgiveness. He also told Hal and Ilona that he wishes to make the trip to the West Coast of North America by ship all around the horn and come up by Los Angeles, San Francisco, to Seattle.

A long but wonderful trip for her father, thought Ilona, but more wonderful would be this visit by her father! Hal and Ilona sat that evening together, closely hanging on to each other and hoping so that this all would come true.

It was now early summer, and after this wet spring and Ilona constantly complaining about it, Hal suggested they take a trip south, through California, and stay a few days in Las Vegas. On the way, they stopped in Reno, not so much for the casinos, but there was a famous bar that had a wonderful collection of rifles on display that

Hal wanted to see. Hal was very much intrigued by old rifles and their history, along with dueling pistols (especially from England), and he would love to start his own collection. Ilona supported her beloved husband in that wish and also started to search for Winchester and Kentucky rifles.

They arrived on the Strip (as it was called) then outside Las Vegas, where Hal had made a reservation at the Dunes Hotel. It was a wide boulevard right outside the town of Las Vegas, with newly built hotels, casinos, beautiful shops, and lots to see. That evening, they took in a wonderful performance by Lionel Hampton and his orchestra. Hal purchased tickets to a late-night performance the next evening.

In the afternoon, both took a nap, since this would be a long afternoon and evening. As they both were sleeping, a loud cracking noise awoke them, and Ilona noticed right away that the beautiful mirror over the dressing table was shattered into thousand pieces. Her concern at first was how do they explain to the management what happened to this mirror.

As they got up quickly from the bed, they both noticed little pieces of wallboard all over the bed. Hal looked around the room and noticed behind the bed on the wall a large hole in the back of the headboard, which had an onionlike dome befitting the hotel's theme, Arabian Nights. Someone in the adjoining room must have taken target practice on their dome, missed, and the bullet came through into Ilona and Hal's room, went clear across, and shattered the mirror.

Hal contacted management, and a security officer came and investigated. They apologized to Hal and Ilona, replaced the mirror, and then secured the room next to theirs so that no one could enter. That party of guests, when they arrived, were taken to the police station.

The next morning, two days early, Hal and Ilona checked out. This was not a place they wanted to spend another night. They drove home, a different way, not inland, by the coast and stopped in San Francisco. They spent two nights there and enjoyed sightseeing and shopping so much that from then on, that was, for many summers, their vacation destination. Even a long weekend for Christmas shopping was thrilling.

On the way home, they took the inland route, not Interstate 101 along the coast. As they approached Oregon, the scenery was getting green and beautiful, and as they drove north, they could see Mount Hood, snow-covered peak glistening in the sunlight. There were some beautiful meadows on the left side of the highway sloping downward and a fence all along the edge.

Hal stopped the car and said, "Would this not be a pretty picture for Friedl, with you standing down by the meadow with Mount Hood in the backdrop?" Ilona agreed, got out of the car, and went down by the fence, taking her pose.

While standing there still and waiting for Hal to take his picture, Ilona suddenly heard a sound. It was a sound she had never heard before but instantly knew what this sound on either side of her presented. Hal must have heard it too and shouted to Ilona, "Stand still!" As he was finishing these two little words, he looked at a streak going by him. It was his Ilona, coming up the hill, crossing the highway, and he heard the car door slamming shut.

When they arrived home and Ilona saw all the beautiful green lawns and lush flowers, she realized that for all this, rain must fall. From this moment on, seeing all the brown hills and dry brown grass on her journey, Ilona so appreciated this state, this green state of Washington, and never ever complained about rain again. She wondered if her darling Hal had planned this trip to be a cure for his beloved Ilona's complaints about the rain.

*   *   *   *

It was 1956, and it was the summer. Ilona's father, August, would visit them and stay awhile, and Hal and Ilona were preparing for August's arrival. Both requested their vacation and were all set with an itinerary to show August all the beautiful sights Seattle and the state of Washington had to offer—mountains (the Cascade

Mountains and the rugged Olympic Mountain Range) and the most beautiful Lake Washington and wonderful saltwater beaches, not to forget, August's wish to see the gorgeous Chevrolet cars up close and personal.

It is Friday evening, and Ilona has just returned from work. The doorbell rang, and she answered, thinking she did not hear a car, and did Hal forget his key? It was a postal employee delivering a telegram she had to sign for. Her heart started beating fast, and she felt so very scared. "Something bad has happened. Otherwise, why a telegram?" Ilona said under her breath. "I wish my dearest Hal would be home. Should I not read it until he does?"

In large black letters, the telegram read, "Vater verstorben, Ich rufe an am Sonntag. Deine Friedl." Ilona read the words aloud and broke down crying. "Father has died, and I will call you on Sunday, Yours Friedl." Ilona does not have to save this telegram for the future; she will always and forever remember these words! Ilona watched for the right time. There is a nine-hour difference between the West Coast and Germany.

During the night, Ilona put a call through to George's office and talked with him. Hal stayed up with his Ilona to give her support, and both waited for the call to come through. George told Ilona that August had an embolism, a blood clot in his heart, and died during his sleep. George found him in bed that morning.

Friedl would call on Sunday, as promised. Ilona of course wanted to be there to support Friedl and also for the funeral. Hal tried to find out what was involved for Ilona to fly back to Germany and, after, coming back into the United States. It was somewhat complicated since Ilona still had a German passport and was not yet a United States citizen. Ilona and Hal had planned for her to go to school in fall and then make the test to become a citizen.

After her arrival in the USA, she had to wait three years to start her citizenship papers. In this present situation, Ilona will need a reentry permit, and that is issued by the American consul in San Francisco, and it will take ten days.

Due to the political turmoil between Russia and the United States at this time, Hal did not want his Ilona to be in Germany if something should start. Ilona needed to have her citizenship before leaving the United States.

On Sunday, the two sisters discussed this issue, and Friedl suggested, "Father won't know if you are here. Why don't you come to Germany after you become a citizen so Hal need not to worry, and in a year, the worst of grieving and mourning is over, and you and I can have a nice visit? I will send you pictures." Friedl added. "Also, the family lawyer wants to try and get Papa buried with Mama and Wolfgang. I am hoping it will be possible so August will be reunited with his Lizzi and with their firstborn. What do you think of that, Ilona?"

Ilona had to swallow a few times, and she could hardly talk, so far away from Friedl, especially right now. She said with tears running down her face, "That would be so nice if all three could make their journey together."

Hal put his arms around his Ilona, held her tight, and let her cry leaning on his chest. Ilona went to sleep after a while. Hal leaned back on the couch pillow and also went to sleep. Would their thoughts and dreams also be one?

August, their father, like his ANMUT, had grace and elegance,

but also showed strength and power.

Lizzi, their mother, much like an heirloom to be loved and cherished,

a delight to everyone, had inner beauty like a flower.

Epilogue

Lizzi's grandson, Friedl's oldest boy, committed suicide in 1977. Friedl was devastated. It was her second child she lost.

Katja's only daughter, Krimhilde, died of cancer in 1997.

Friedl's third child, her son Rainald, died of pneumonia in 2000.

Katja, Lizzi's youngest sister, died from a broken heart in 2002.

Friedl's dear husband, George, died of a broken heart after he had lost all his children in 2004.

Friedl, after a long struggle with cancer, Ilona and Hal by her side, died in 2007.

Ilona's love, Hal, due to complications with Parkinson's disease, died in January of 2017, his Ilona by his side, holding him.

No one is left of the family except Ilona, the youngest of Lizzi, the general's bride.

Edwards Brothers Inc.
Ann Arbor MI. USA
December 12, 2017